ESPete® in ESPresident

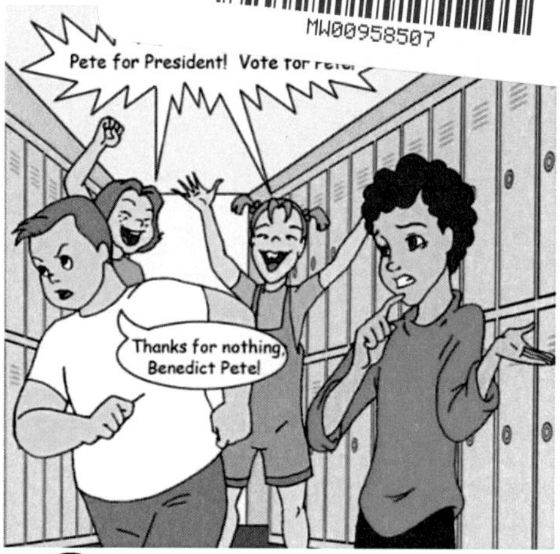
Pete for President! Vote
Thanks for nothing, Benedict Pete!

Written by Arnold Rudnick
Illustrated by Marcelo Gorenman

featuring

ESPete's PSYCHIC JOKE BOOK

ESPete® in ESPresident
featuring ESPete's Psychic Joke Book

Paraphrase, LLC
P.O. Box 56508
Sherman Oaks, CA 91413
paraphrasellc.com

Read a Book, Read a Mind ®

ISBN-13: 978-0-9815879-3-6

Library of Congress Control Number: 2015919009
Printed in the United States of America
First Printing: **December 2015**

Special Thanks

Loyd Auerbach
Kevin Cleary
Doina Paraschiv
Puzzle-Maker.com
Sam Yoon
and… You Know

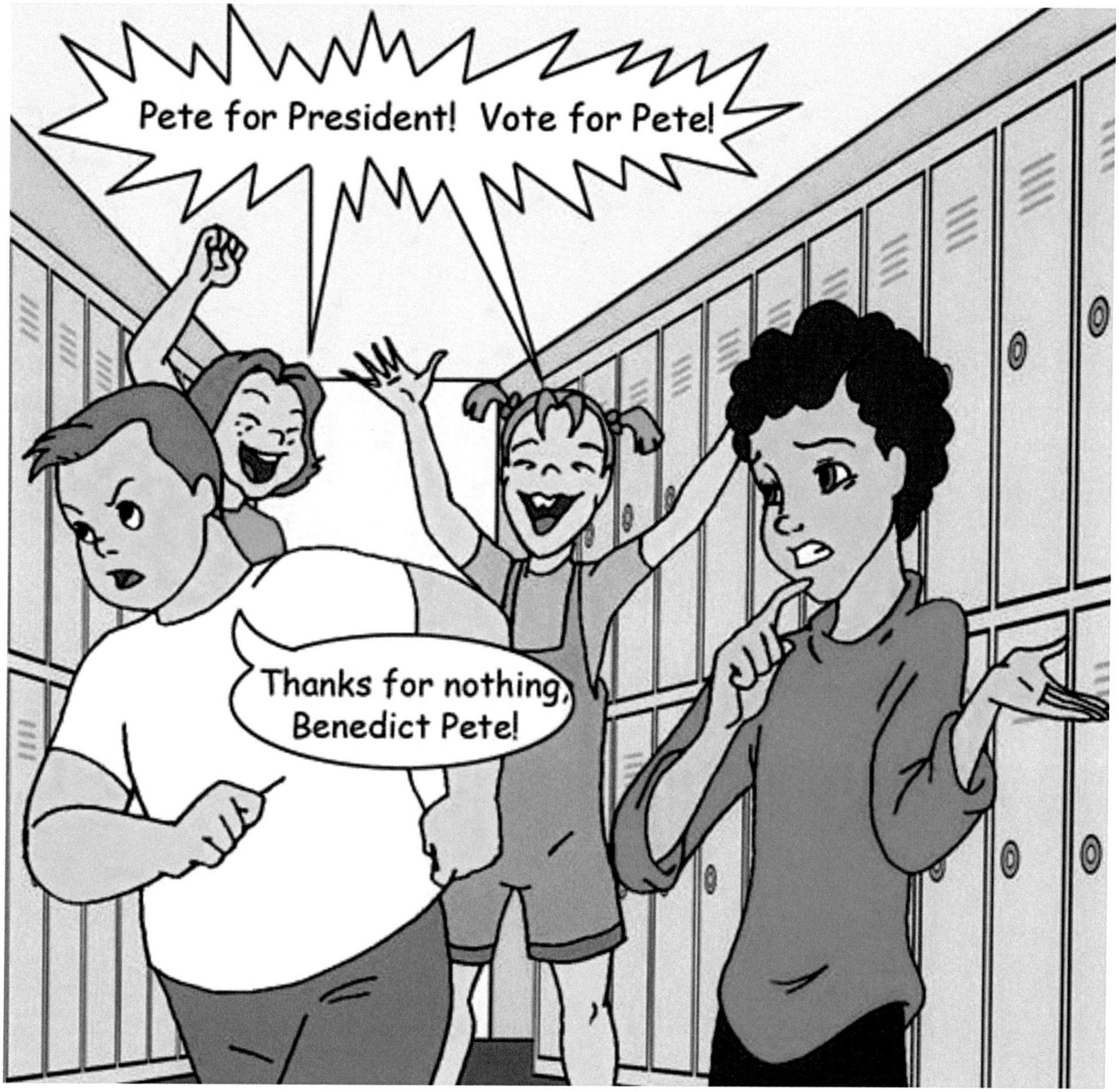
Pete for President! Vote for Pete!
Thanks for nothing, Benedict Pete!

ESPete® in ESPresident

The Perils of a Paranormal Preteen

Pete Powell is a sixth grader with Extrasensory Perception (ESP), also called the Sixth Sense. He can read minds, an ability known as **Telepathy**, but that skill gets him into trouble as often as not. Other ESP talents include: **Clairvoyance**, an awareness of objects and events hidden from the normal senses of hearing, sight, smell, taste and touch; and **Precognition**, awareness of objects or events in the future. Cool, yes. Complicated, no doubt.

Rodney, the school bully, figured out Pete can read minds, and calls him E.S. Pete. They're almost, kinda, sorta friends, which is admittedly better than getting beat up, but Rodney isn't always patient enough to understand Pete's talents don't come with an on/off switch.

Casey doesn't know about Pete's psychic gift, and Pete would like to keep it that way. After all, he has a huge crush on her. Reading her mind may not help win her heart, but he's worried she might freak out if she knew he knew what she knew.

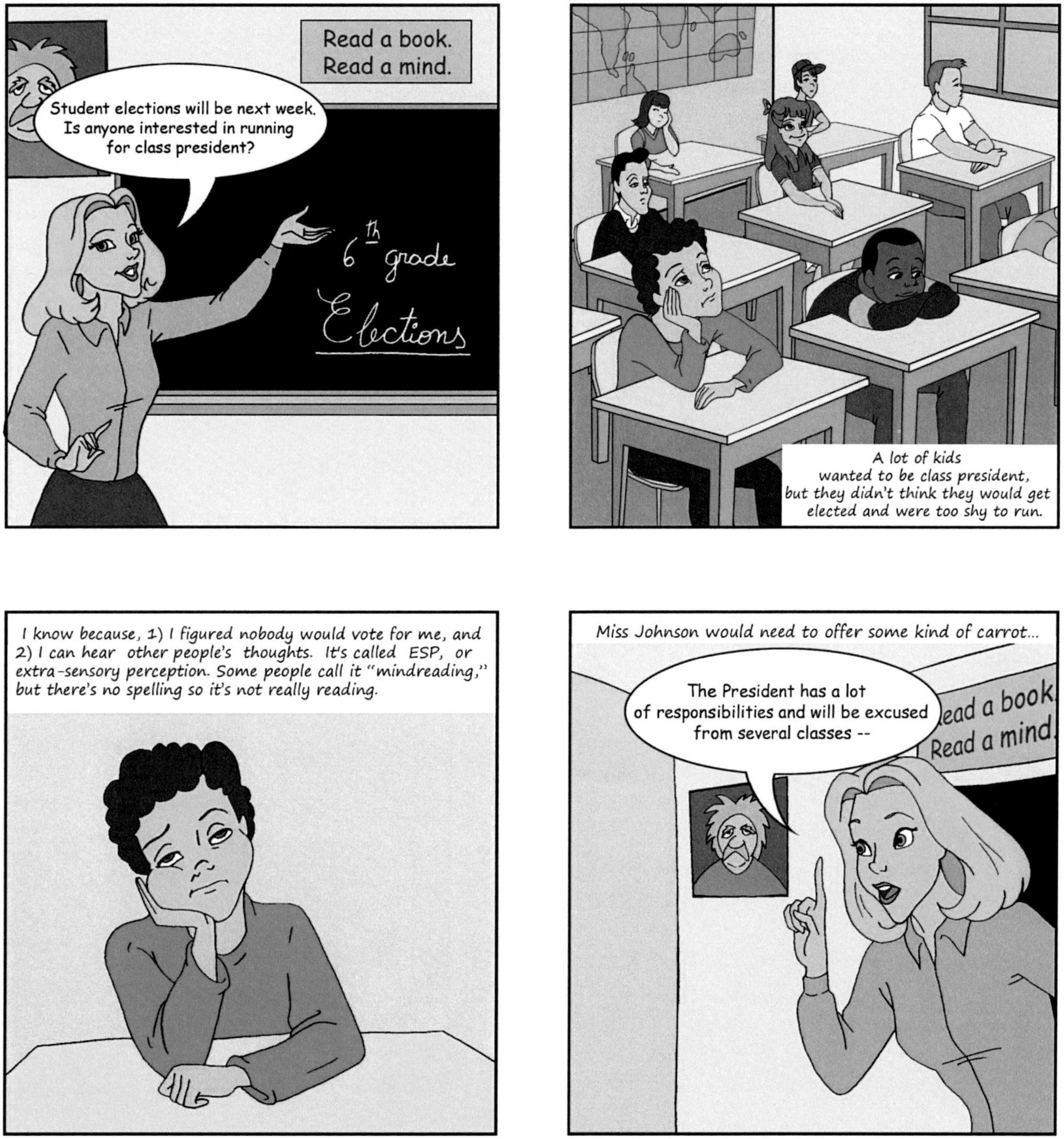

Read a book.
Read a mind.
Student elections will be next week. Is anyone interested in running for class president?
6th grade
Elections
A lot of kids wanted to be class president, but they didn't think they would get elected and were too shy to run.
I know because, 1) I figured nobody would vote for me, and 2) I can hear other people's thoughts. It's called ESP, or extra-sensory perception. Some people call it "mindreading," but there's no spelling so it's not really reading.
Miss Johnson would need to offer some kind of carrot...
The President has a lot of responsibilities and will be excused from several classes --
ead a book
Read a mind

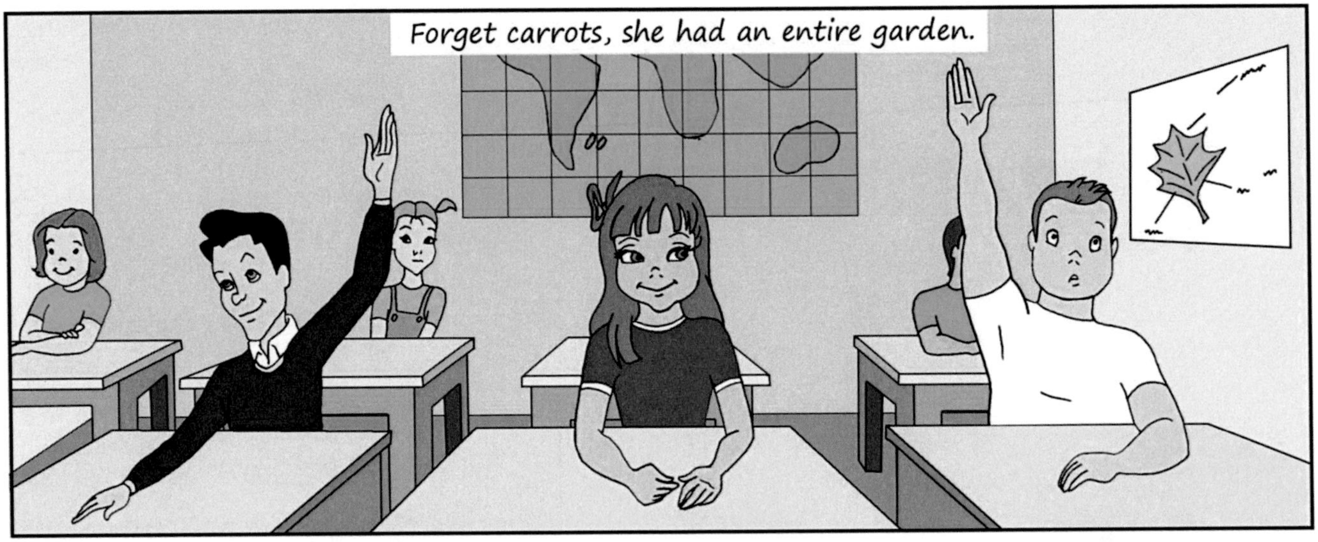
Forget carrots, she had an entire garden.

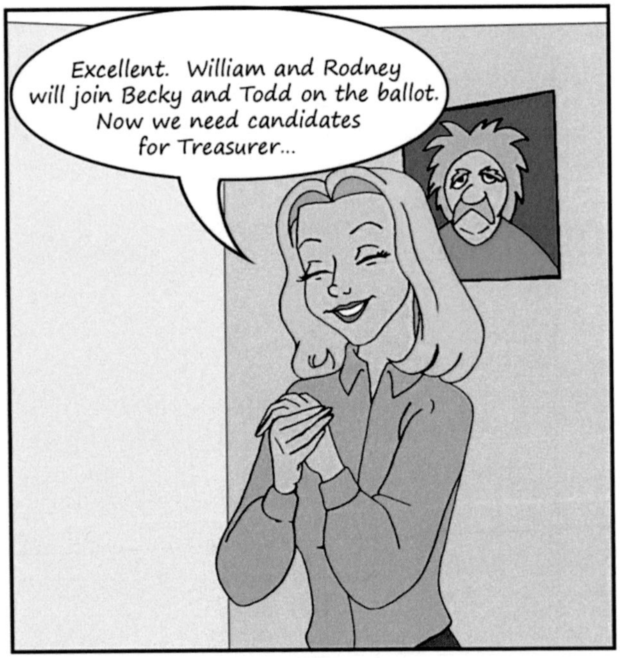
Excellent. William and Rodney will join Becky and Todd on the ballot. Now we need candidates for Treasurer...

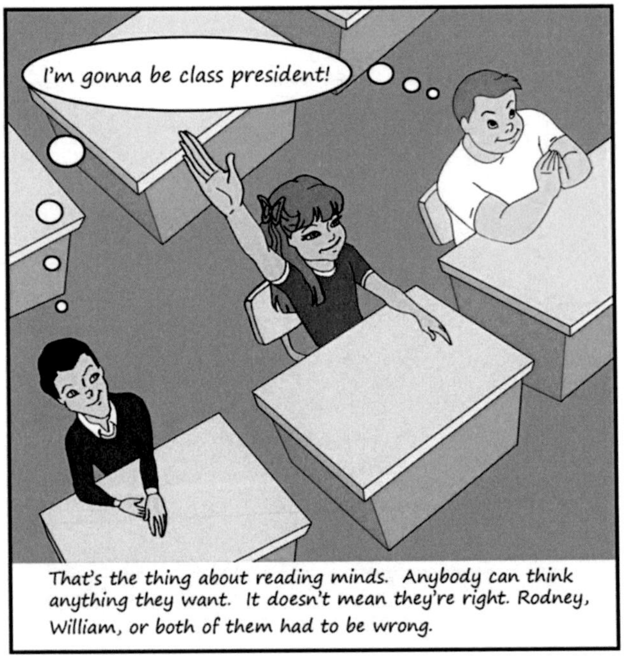
I'm gonna be class president!
That's the thing about reading minds. Anybody can think anything they want. It doesn't mean they're right. Rodney, William, or both of them had to be wrong.

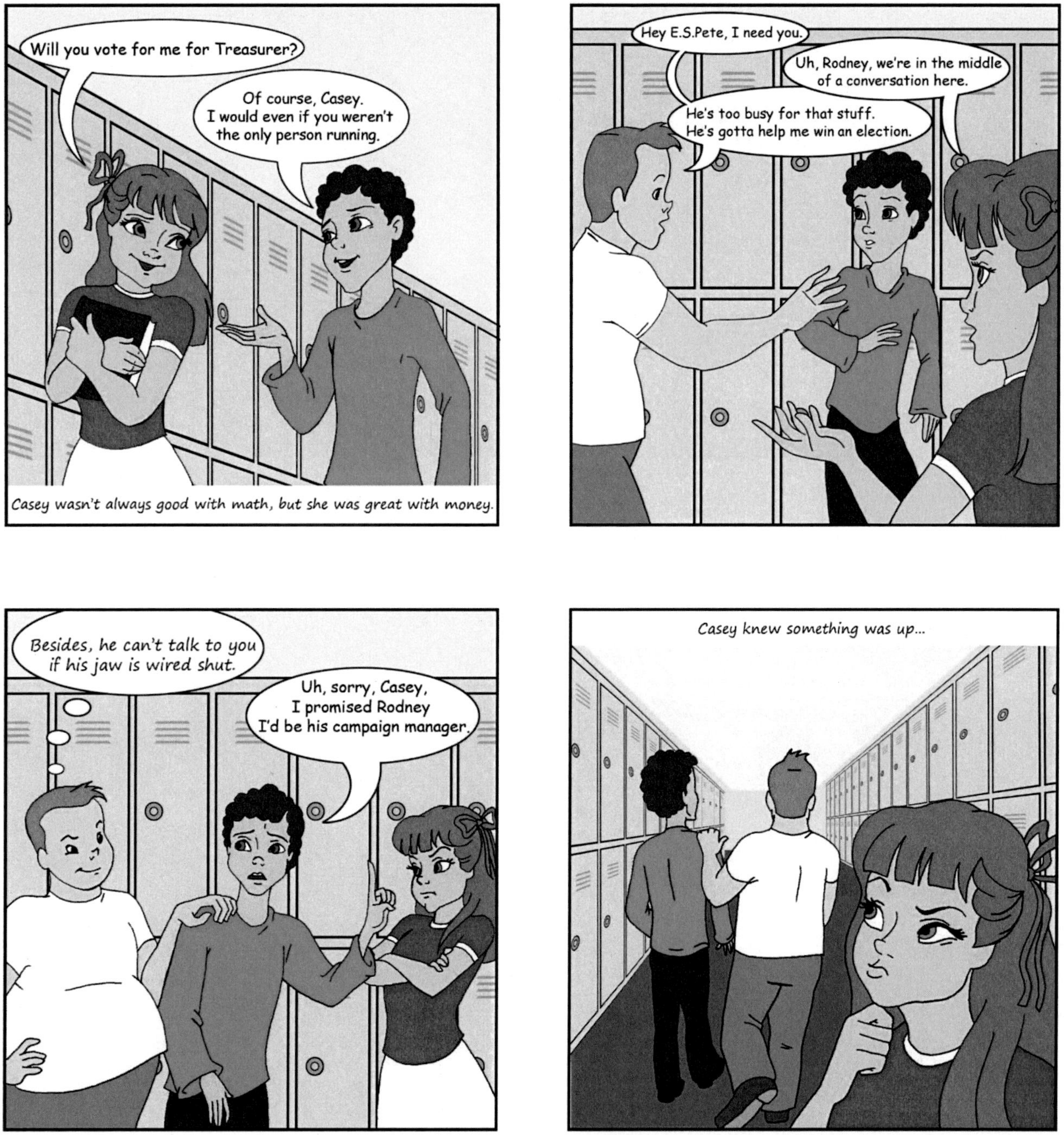
Will you vote for me for Treasurer?
Of course, Casey. I would even if you weren't the only person running.
Casey wasn't always good with math, but she was great with money.
Hey E.S.Pete, I need you.
Uh, Rodney, we're in the middle of a conversation here.
He's too busy for that stuff. He's gotta help me win an election.
Besides, he can't talk to you if his jaw is wired shut.
Uh, sorry, Casey, I promised Rodney I'd be his campaign manager.
Casey knew something was up...

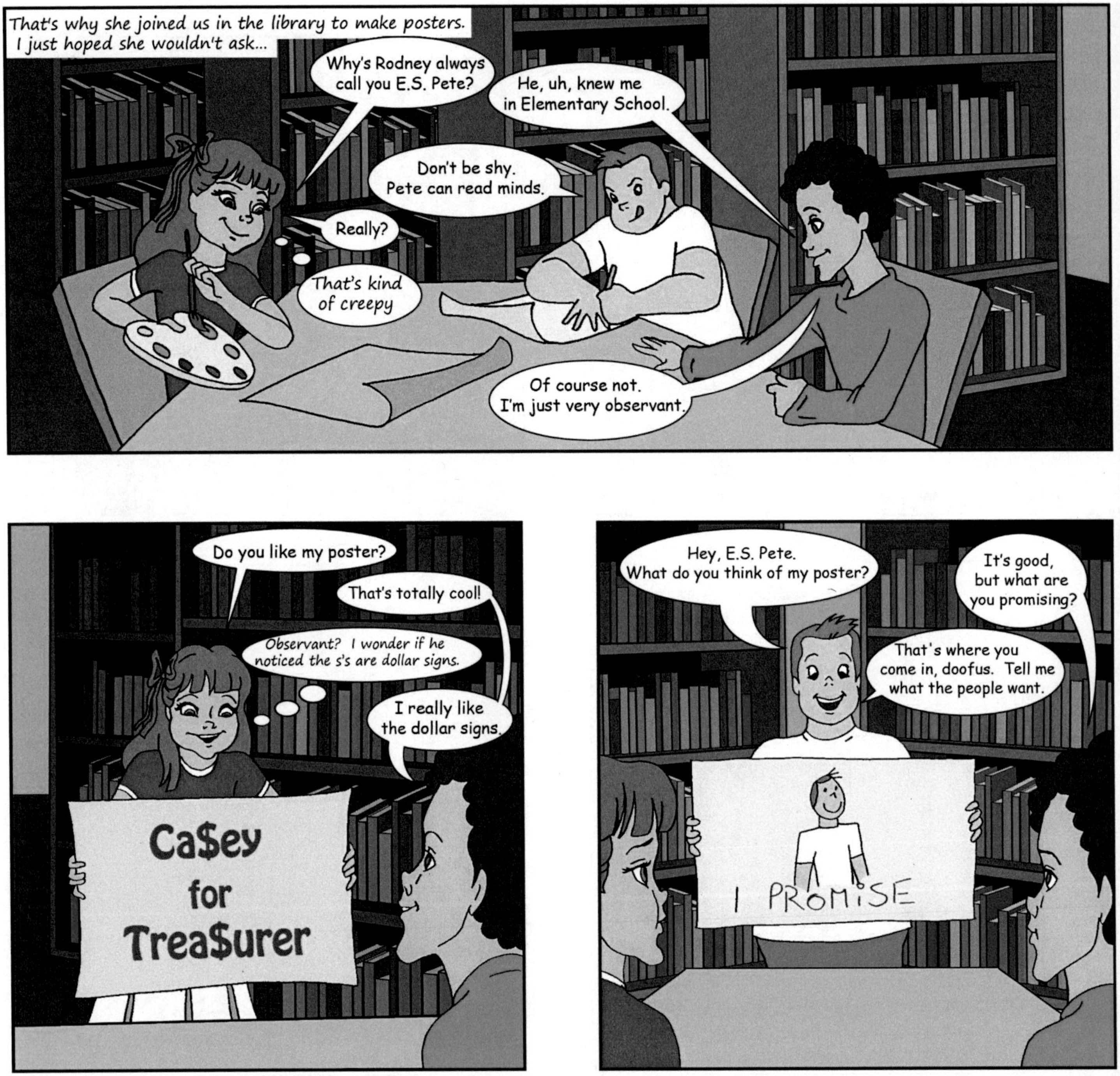
That's why she joined us in the library to make posters.
I just hoped she wouldn't ask...
Why's Rodney always call you E.S. Pete?
He, uh, knew me in Elementary School.
Don't be shy. Pete can read minds.
Really?
That's kind of creepy
Of course not. I'm just very observant.
Do you like my poster?
That's totally cool!
Observant? I wonder if he noticed the s's are dollar signs.
I really like the dollar signs.
Ca$ey
for
Trea$urer
Hey, E.S. Pete. What do you think of my poster?
It's good, but what are you promising?
That's where you come in, doofus. Tell me what the people want.
I PROMISE

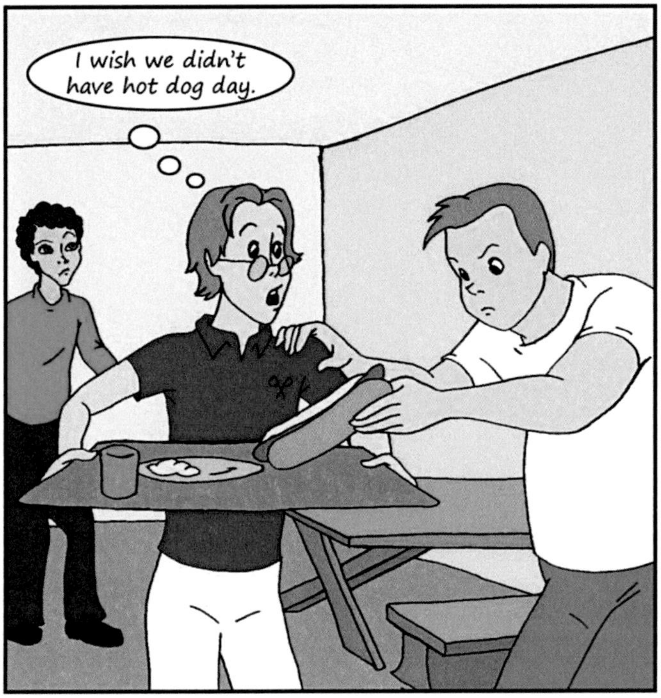
I wish we didn't
have hot dog day.

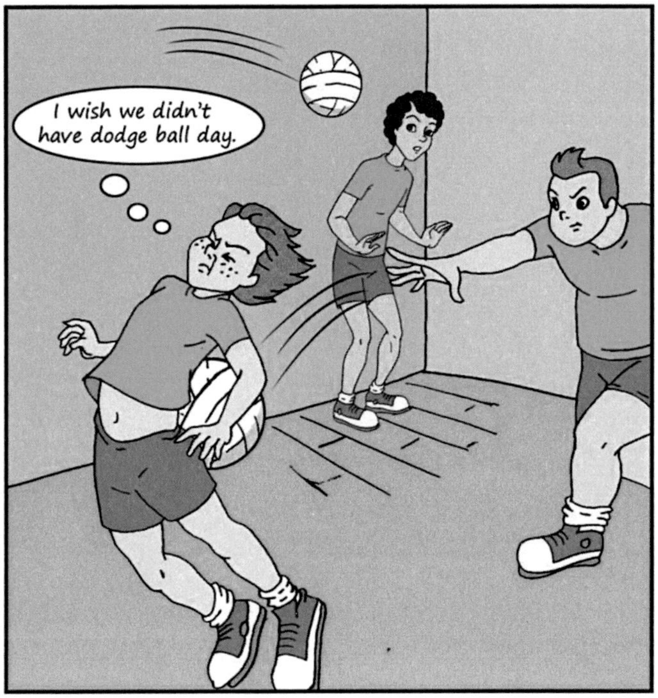
I wish we didn't
have dodge ball day.

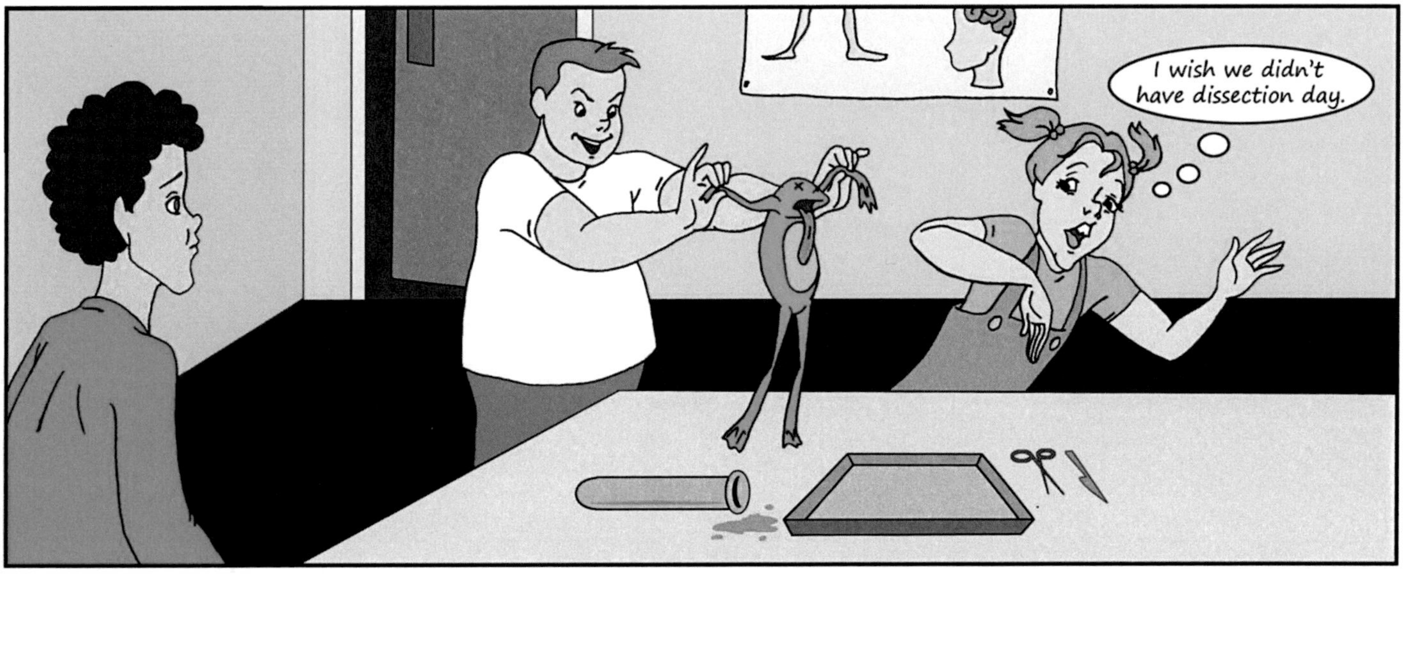
I wish we didn't
have dissection day.

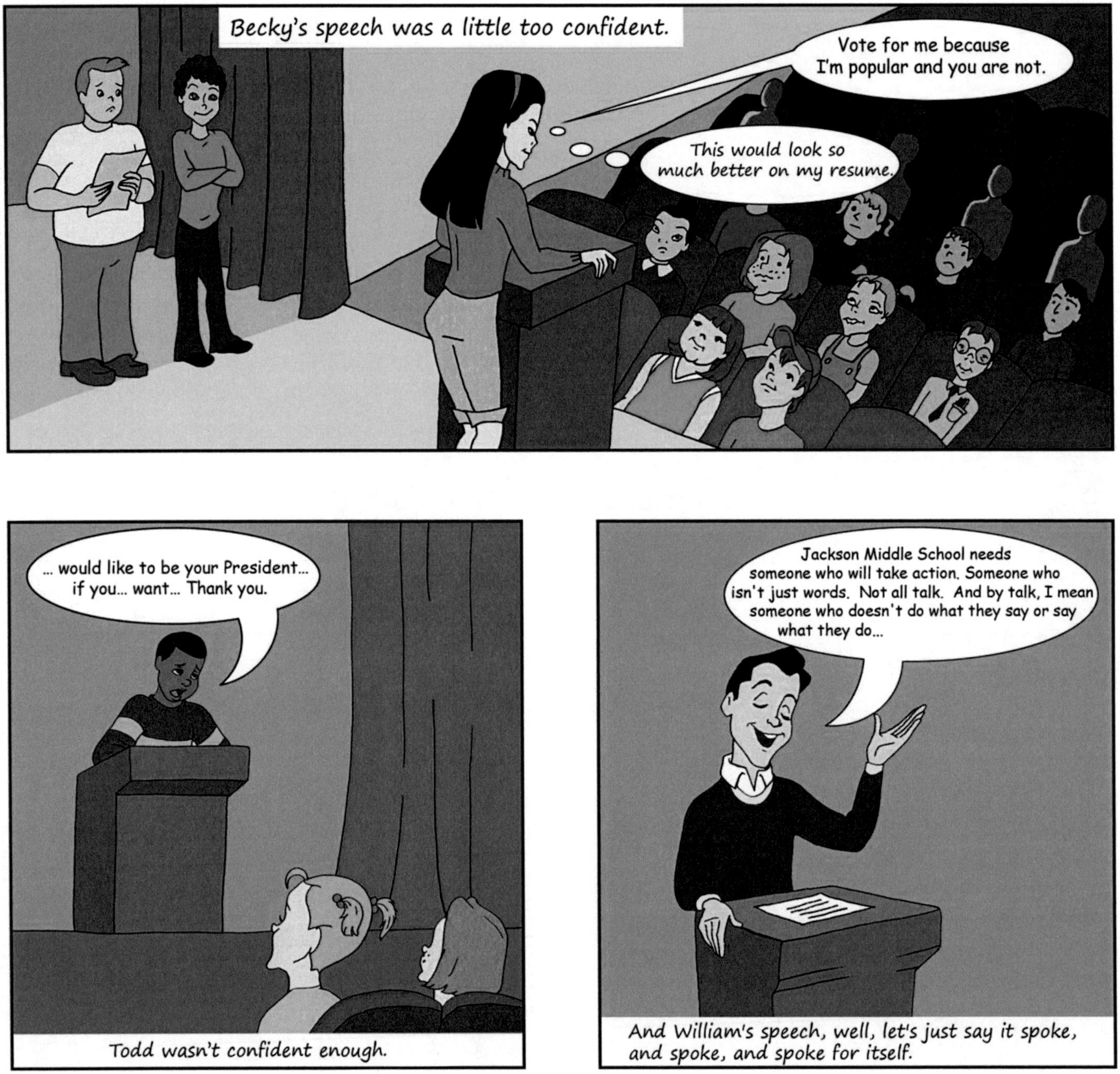
Becky's speech was a little too confident.
Vote for me because I'm popular and you are not.
This would look so much better on my resume.
... would like to be your President... if you... want... Thank you.
Todd wasn't confident enough.
Jackson Middle School needs someone who will take action. Someone who isn't just words. Not all talk. And by talk, I mean someone who doesn't do what they say or say what they do...
And William's speech, well, let's just say it spoke, and spoke, and spoke for itself.

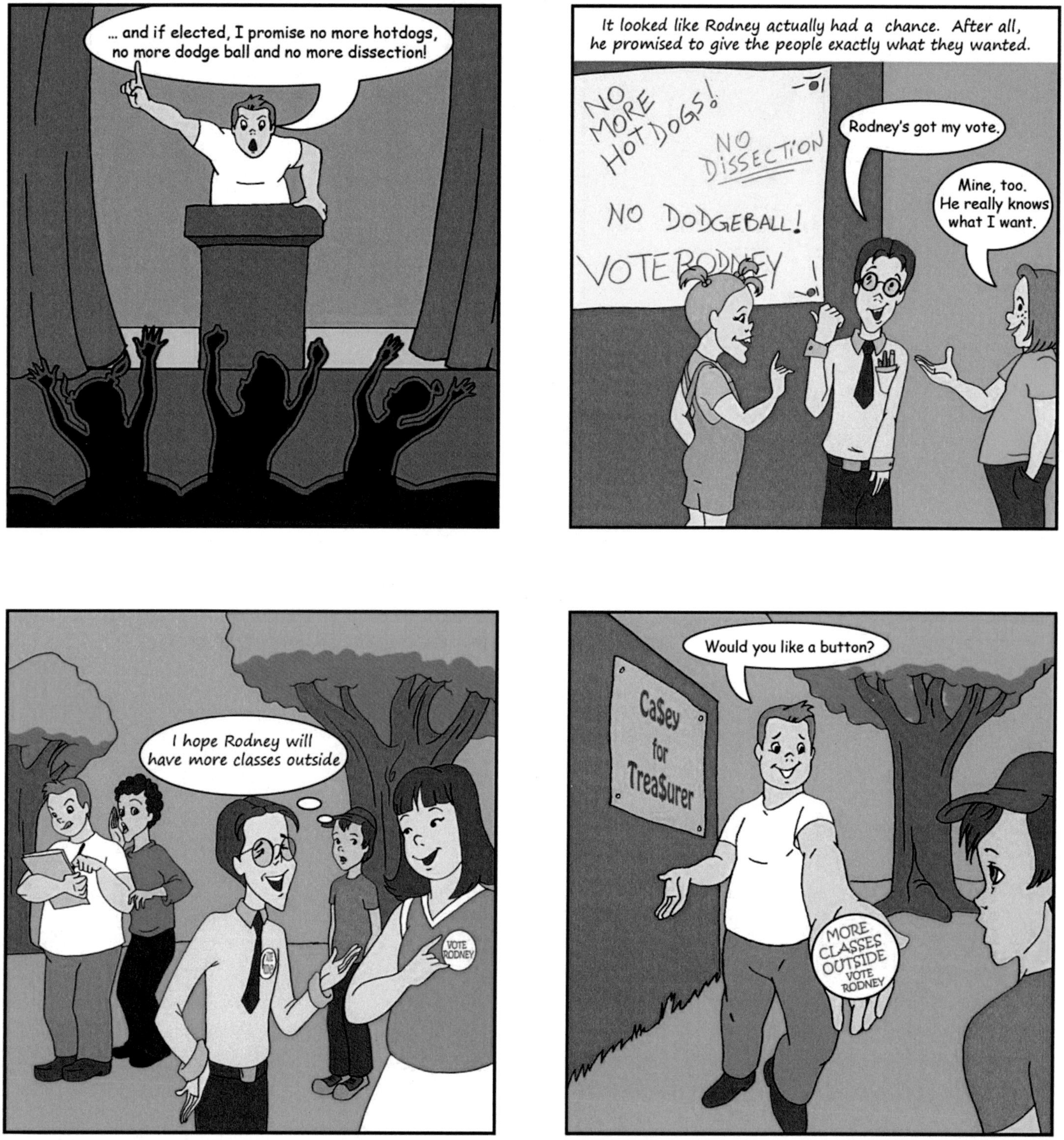

... and if elected, I promise no more hotdogs, no more dodge ball and no more dissection!
It looked like Rodney actually had a chance. After all, he promised to give the people exactly what they wanted.
NO MORE HOT DOGS!
NO DISSECTION
NO DODGEBALL!
VOTE RODNEY !
Rodney's got my vote.
Mine, too. He really knows what I want.
I hope Rodney will have more classes outside
VOTE RODNEY
Would you like a button?
CaSey for TreaSurer
MORE CLASSES OUTSIDE VOTE RODNEY

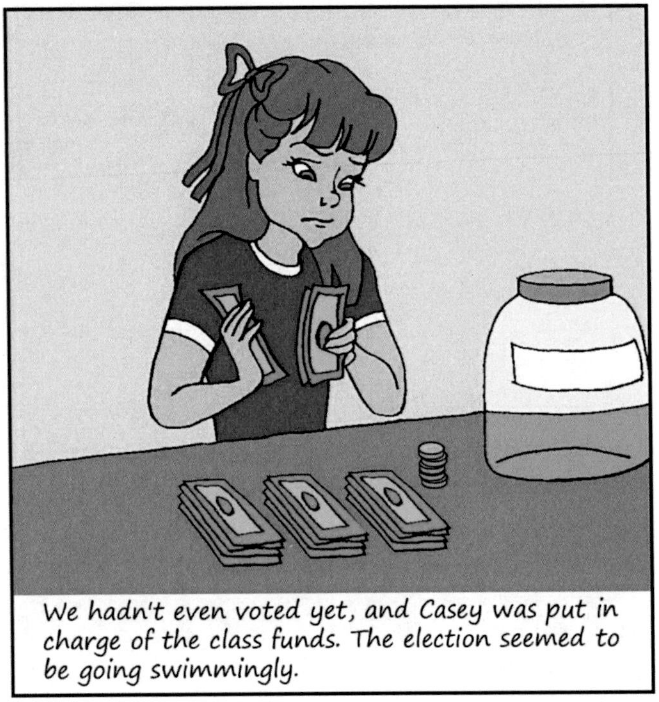
We hadn't even voted yet, and Casey was put in charge of the class funds. The election seemed to be going swimmingly.

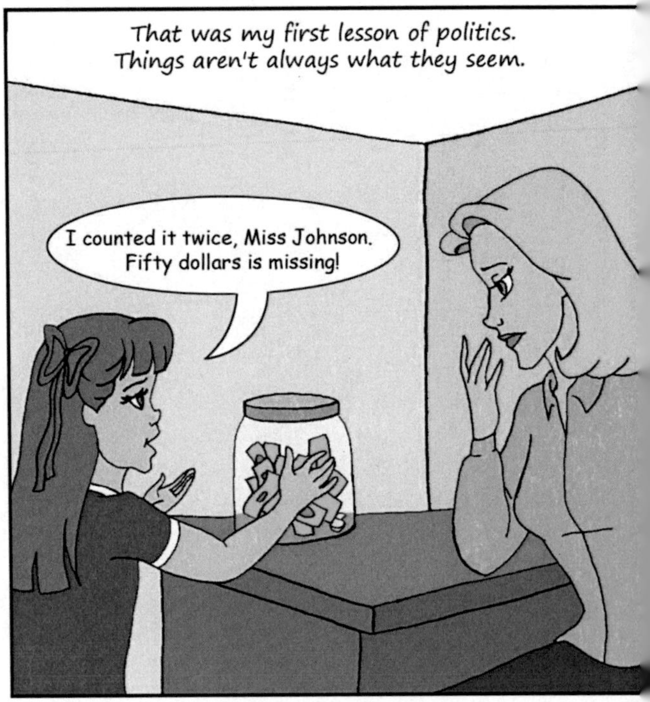
That was my first lesson of politics. Things aren't always what they seem.
I counted it twice, Miss Johnson. Fifty dollars is missing!

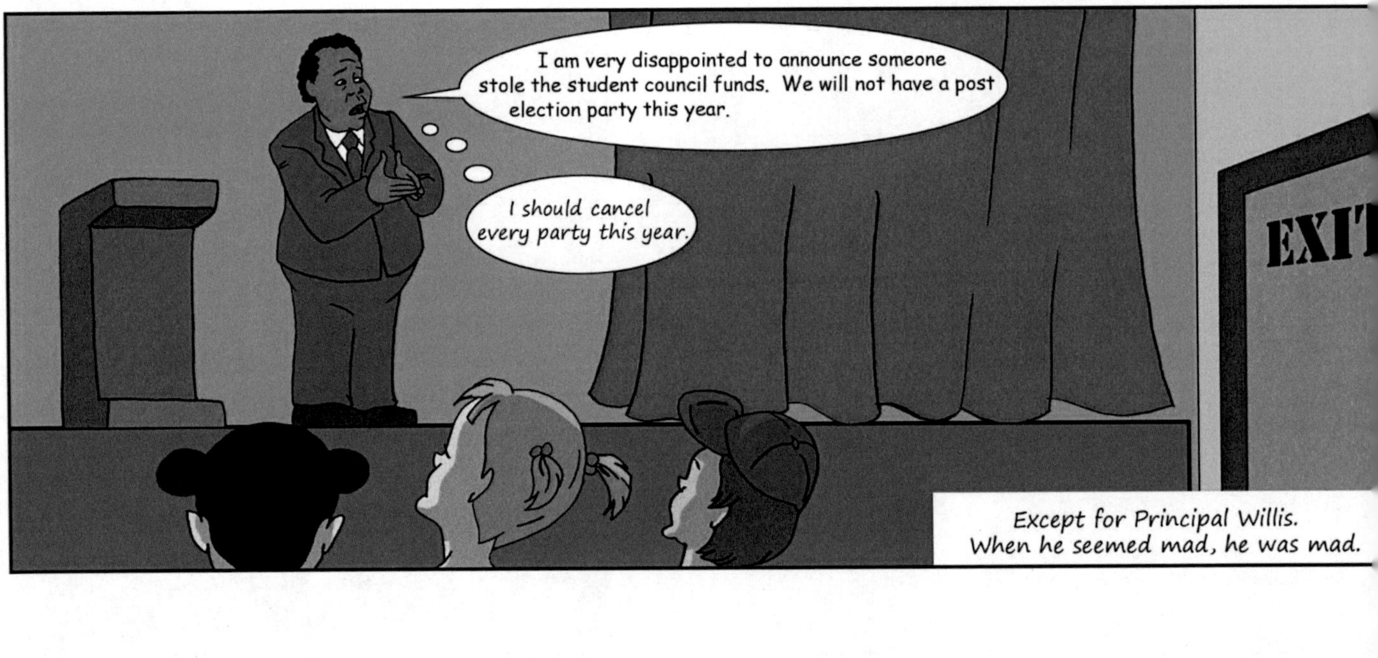
I am very disappointed to announce someone stole the student council funds. We will not have a post election party this year.
I should cancel every party this year.
EXIT
Except for Principal Willis. When he seemed mad, he was mad.

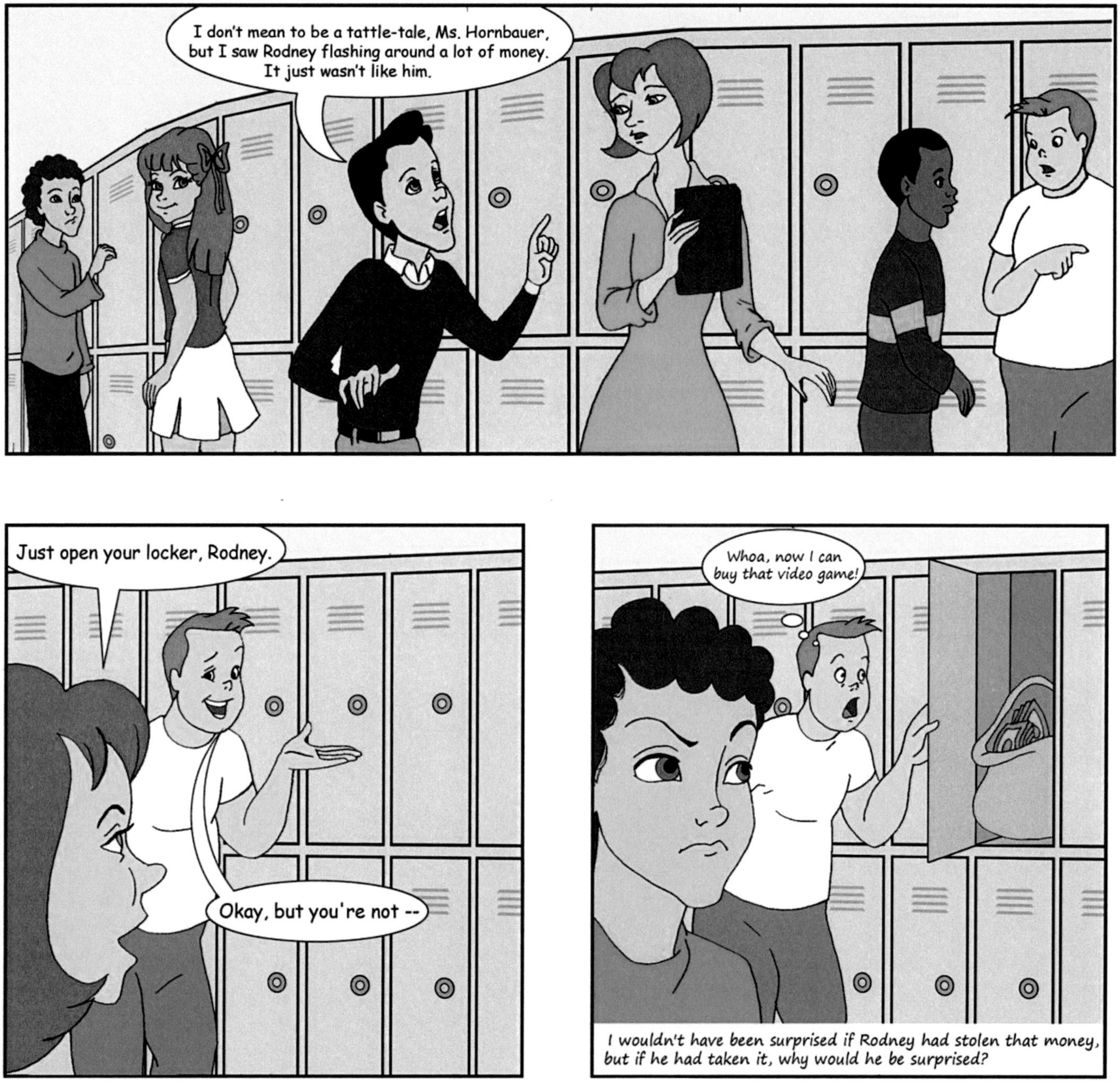
I don't mean to be a tattle-tale, Ms. Hornbauer, but I saw Rodney flashing around a lot of money. It just wasn't like him.
Just open your locker, Rodney.
Okay, but you're not --
Whoa, now I can buy that video game!
I wouldn't have been surprised if Rodney had stolen that money, but if he had taken it, why would he be surprised?

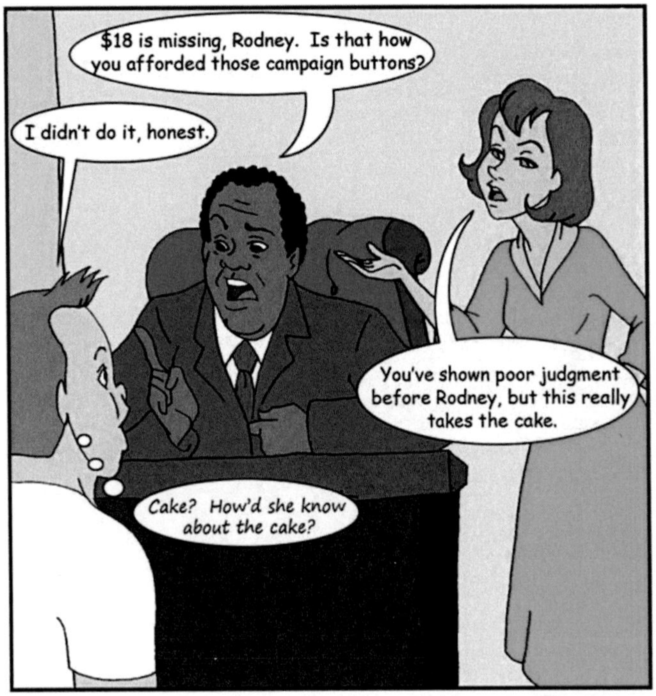
$18 is missing, Rodney. Is that how you afforded those campaign buttons?
I didn't do it, honest.
You've shown poor judgment before Rodney, but this really takes the cake.
Cake? How'd she know about the cake?

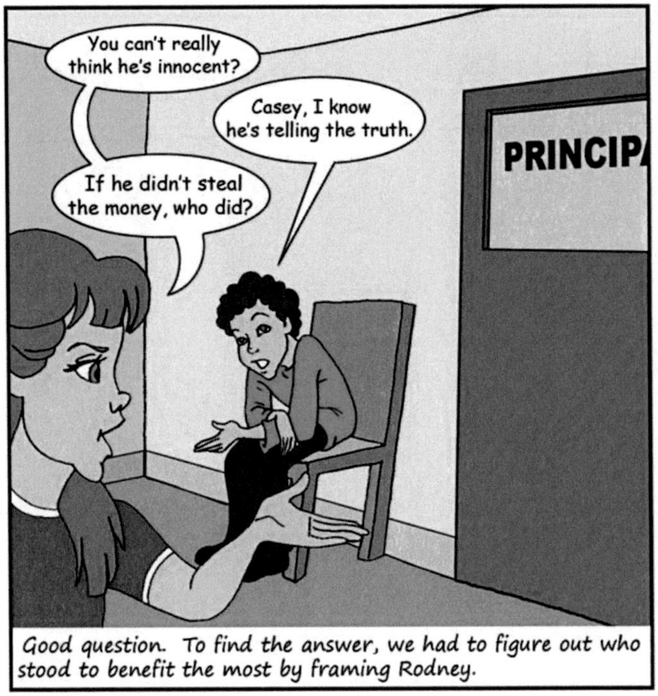
You can't really think he's innocent?
Casey, I know he's telling the truth.
If he didn't steal the money, who did?
PRINCIPA
Good question. To find the answer, we had to figure out who stood to benefit the most by framing Rodney.

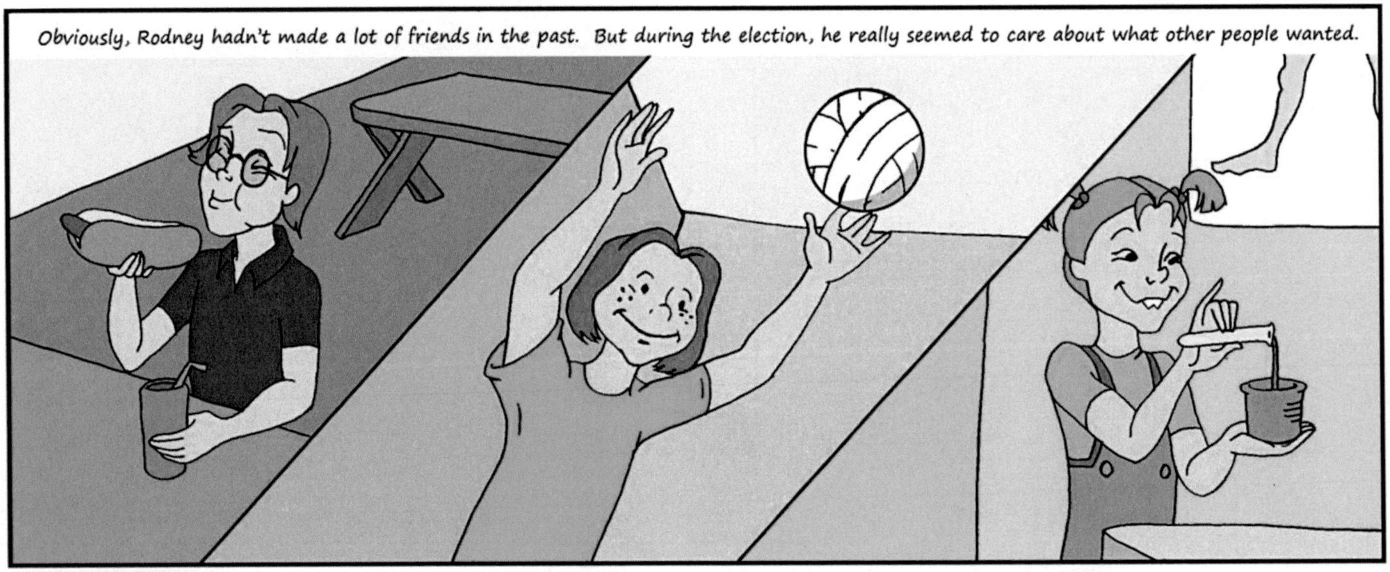
Obviously, Rodney hadn't made a lot of friends in the past. But during the election, he really seemed to care about what other people wanted.

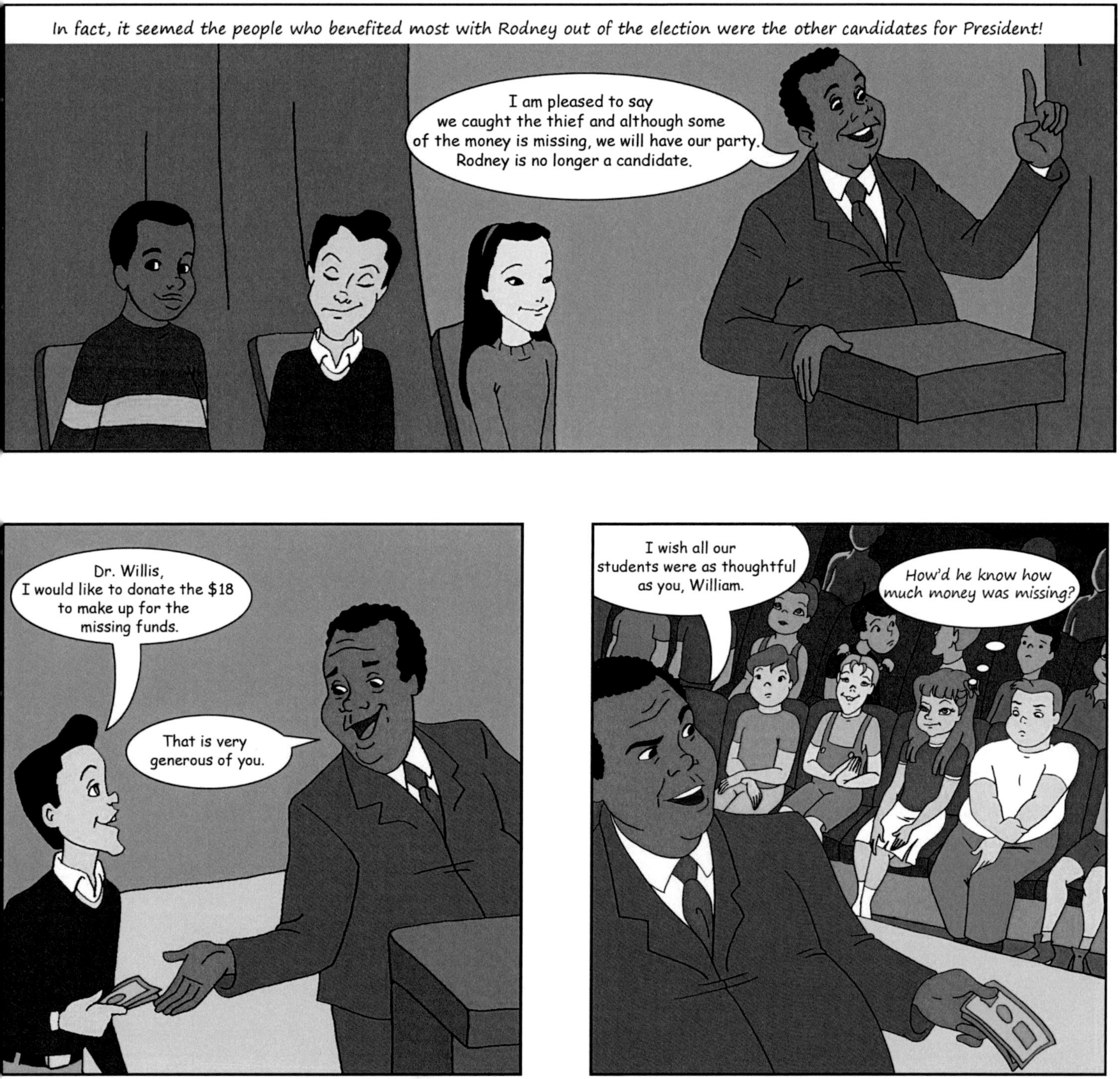
In fact, it seemed the people who benefited most with Rodney out of the election were the other candidates for President!
I am pleased to say we caught the thief and although some of the money is missing, we will have our party. Rodney is no longer a candidate.
Dr. Willis, I would like to donate the $18 to make up for the missing funds.
That is very generous of you.
I wish all our students were as thoughtful as you, William.
How'd he know how much money was missing?

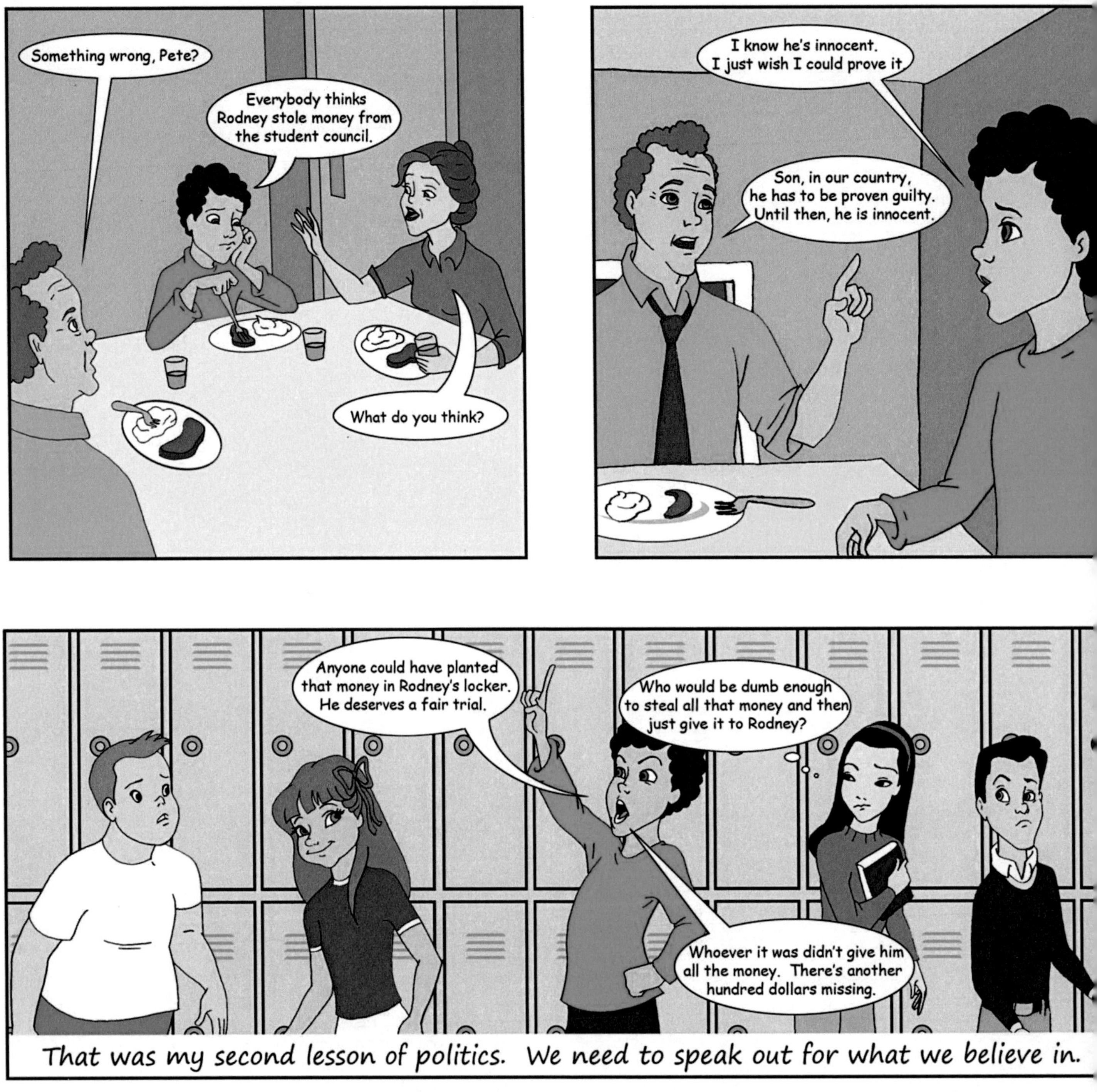
Something wrong, Pete?
Everybody thinks Rodney stole money from the student council.
What do you think?
I know he's innocent. I just wish I could prove it.
Son, in our country, he has to be proven guilty. Until then, he is innocent.
Anyone could have planted that money in Rodney's locker. He deserves a fair trial.
Who would be dumb enough to steal all that money and then just give it to Rodney?
Whoever it was didn't give him all the money. There's another hundred dollars missing.
That was my second lesson of politics. We need to speak out for what we believe in.

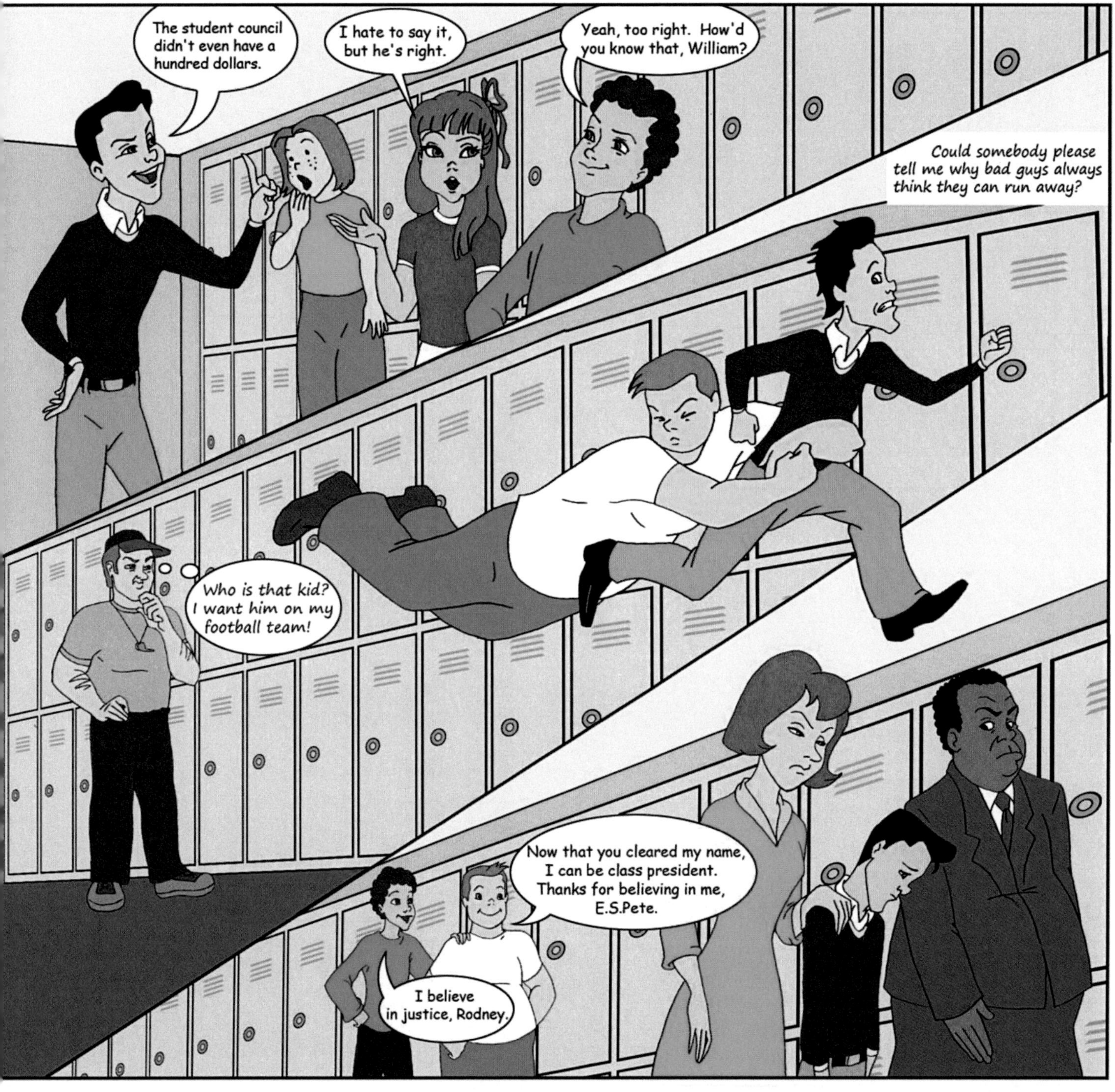

The student council didn't even have a hundred dollars.
I hate to say it, but he's right.
Yeah, too right. How'd you know that, William?
Could somebody please tell me why bad guys always think they can run away?
Who is that kid? I want him on my football team!
Now that you cleared my name, I can be class president. Thanks for believing in me, E.S.Pete.
I believe in justice, Rodney.

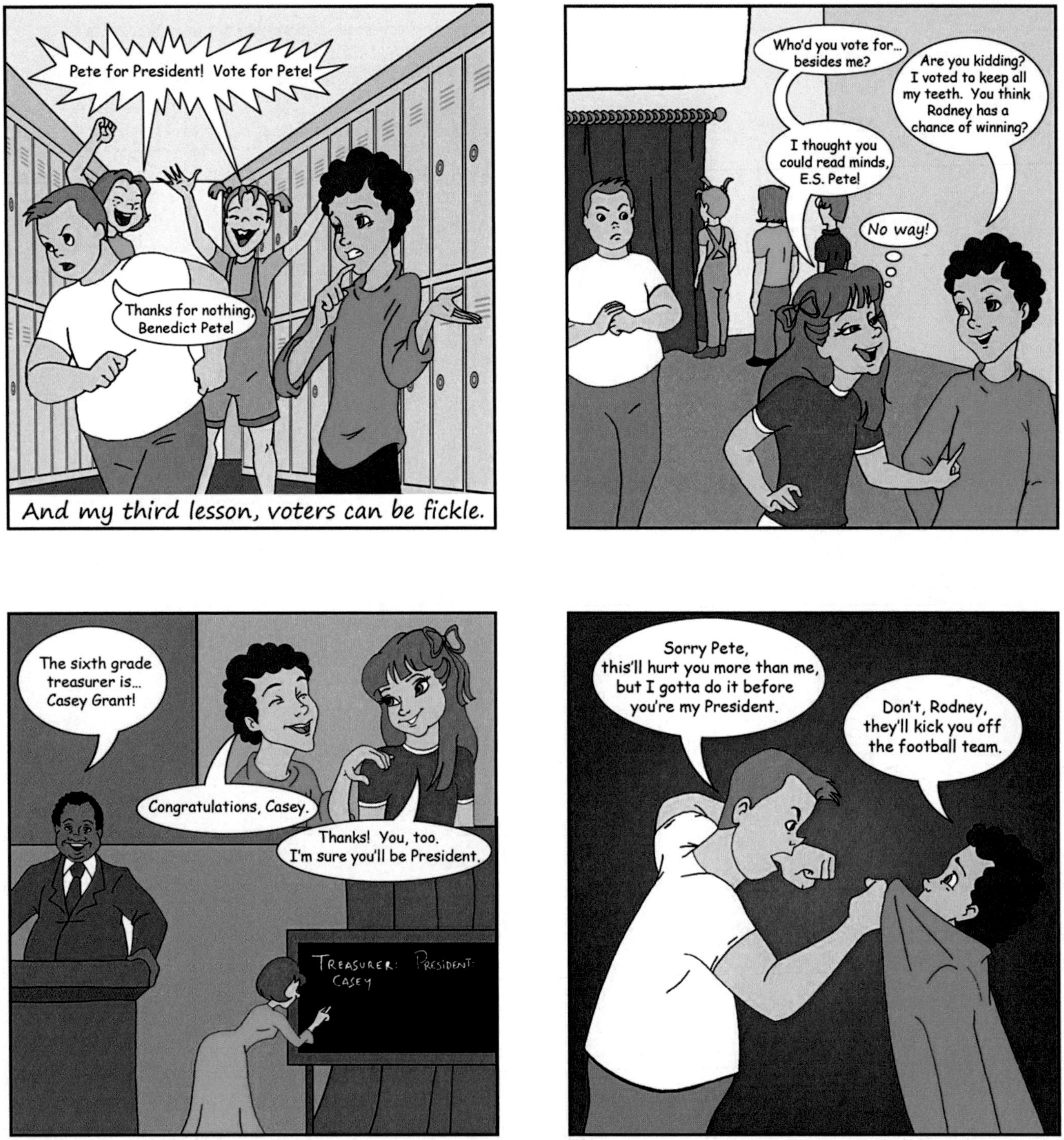
Pete for President! Vote for Pete!
Thanks for nothing, Benedict Pete!
And my third lesson, voters can be fickle.
Who'd you vote for... besides me?
I thought you could read minds, E.S. Pete!
Are you kidding? I voted to keep all my teeth. You think Rodney has a chance of winning?
No way!
The sixth grade treasurer is... Casey Grant!
Congratulations, Casey.
Thanks! You, too. I'm sure you'll be President.
TREASURER: PRESIDENT:
CASEY
Sorry Pete, this'll hurt you more than me, but I gotta do it before you're my President.
Don't, Rodney, they'll kick you off the football team.

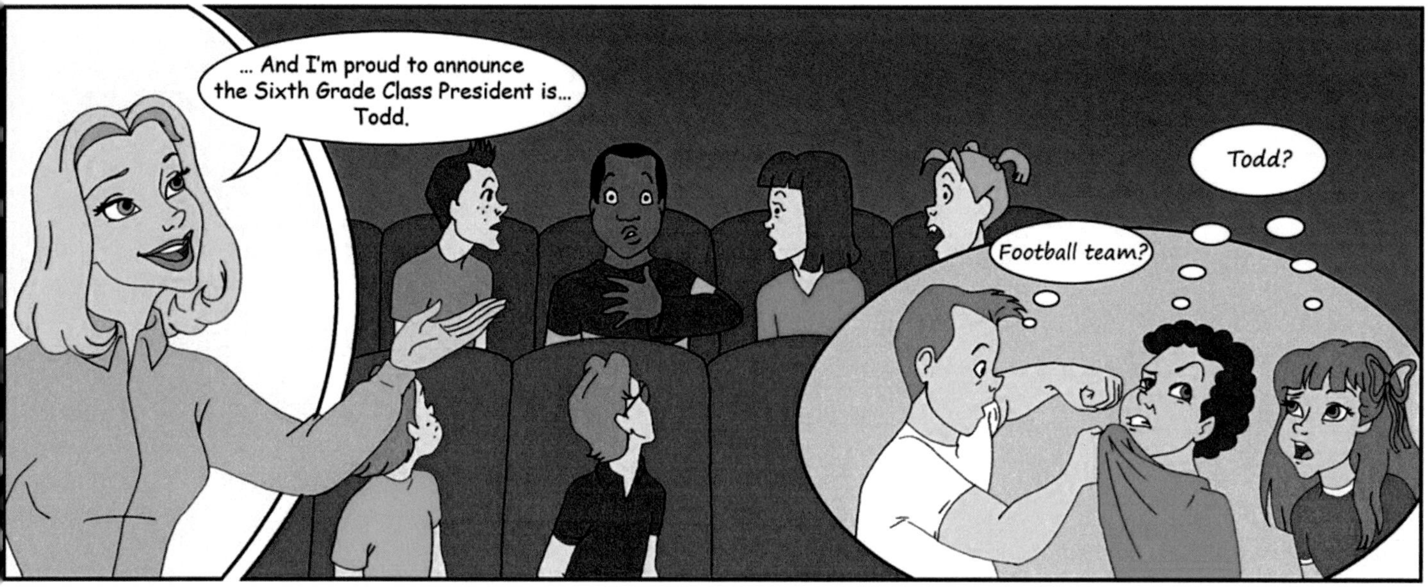
... And I'm proud to announce the Sixth Grade Class President is... Todd.
Football team?
Todd?

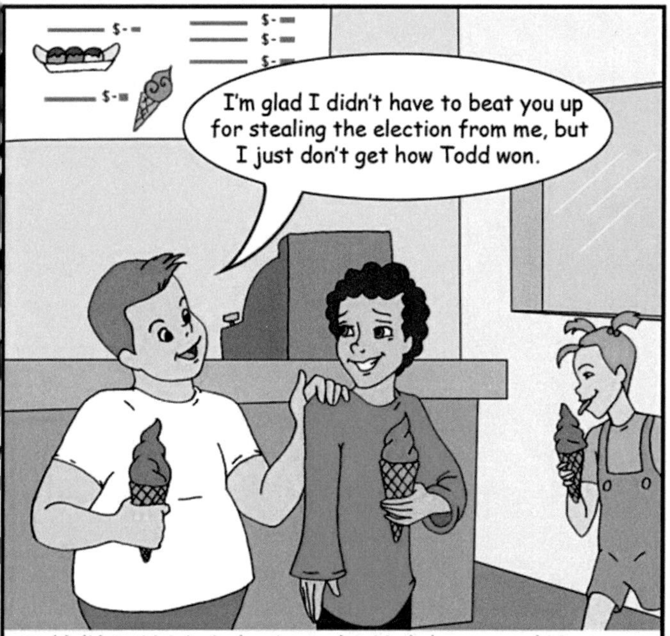
I'm glad I didn't have to beat you up for stealing the election from me, but I just don't get how Todd won.

Todd didn't think he had a chance, but his dad encouraged him to run. And since the school president's biggest responsibility is planning all the big celebrations, he really was the most qualified.

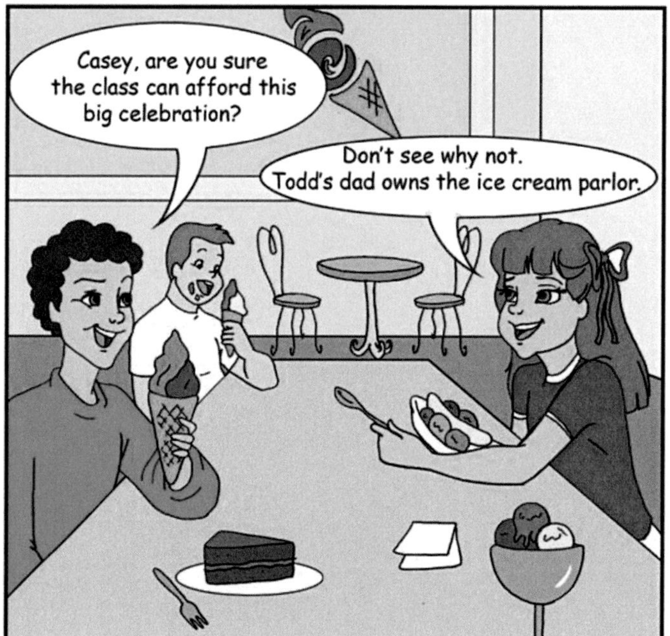
Casey, are you sure the class can afford this big celebration?
Don't see why not. Todd's dad owns the ice cream parlor.

In the end, the Jackson Middle School vote came down to the old party lines: Chocolate or Vanilla.

The End

PSYCHIC CROSSWORD PUZZLE

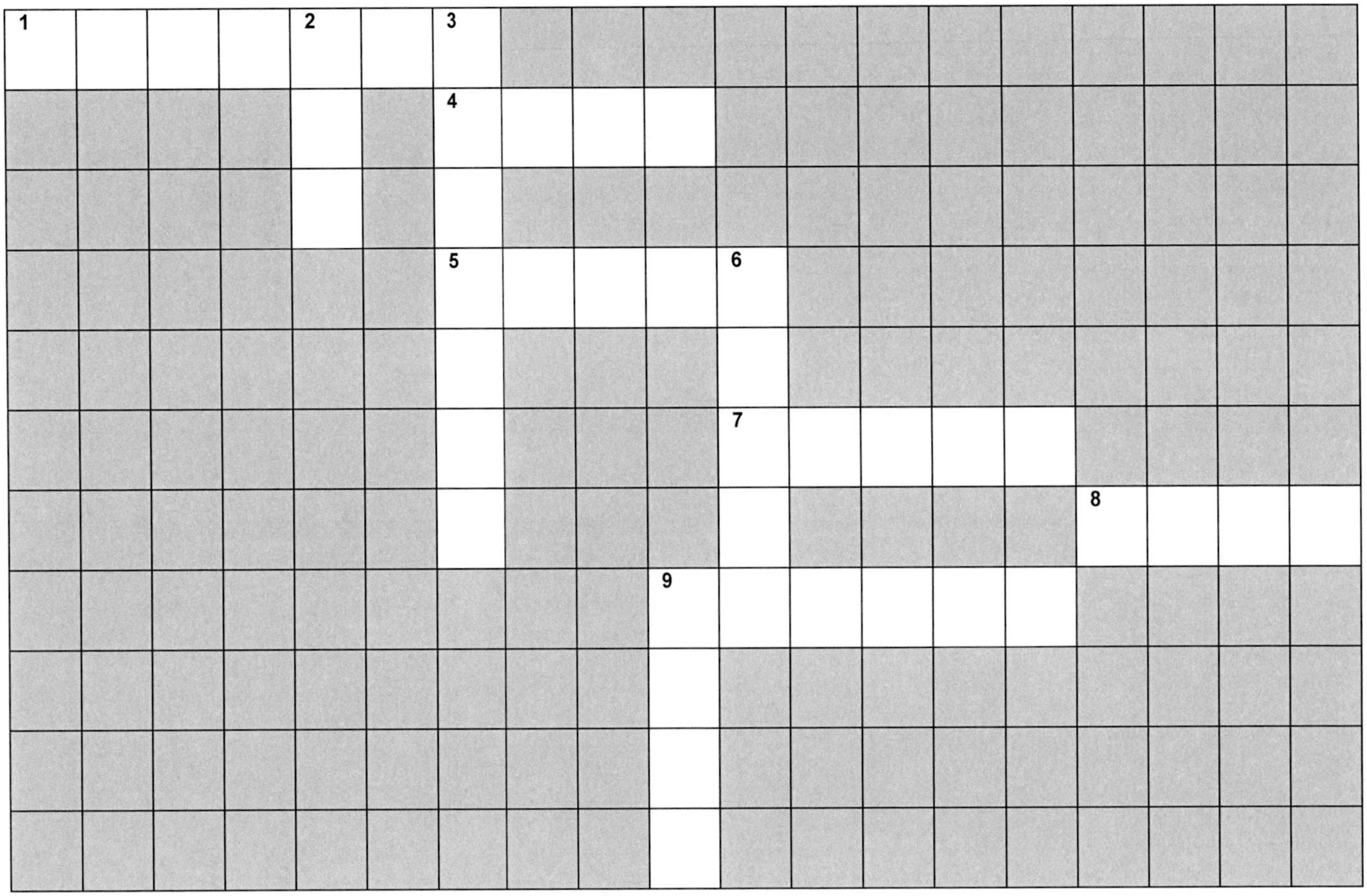

ACROSS

1 Touch may use these
4 Hearing uses these
5 The sense that uses Eyes
7 The sense that uses your Nose
8 Read a ____, Read a Mind®
9 Small, ______, or Large

DOWN

2 The Sixth Sense
3 S in ESPete®
6 The tongue's sense
9 Telepathy moves objects with this

(answers on last page)

PSYCHIC WORD SEARCH

```
E S P R E S I D E N T
P G Y Q C M C G R R R
N A J H N I E A E P B
Y Z R N T Y H D S Y Z
E E N A M A A C I E L
S D N J N E P E Y U Y
P Y Y D R O S E L S M
R B L D O P R M L G P
L L N M E R B M V E Z
N I D T Q P R P A Z T
M K E N N L Y W J L X
```

CAN YOU FIND THESE WORDS IN THE PUZZLE?

___	CASEY	___	MINDREADER
___	ESP	___	PARANORMAL
___	ESPETE	___	PSYCHIC
___	ESPRESIDENT	___	RODNEY
___	MEDIUM	___	TELEPATHY

Find 1-3 Words   Excellent
Find 4-7 Words   S u p e r b
Find 8-10 Words   Perfect
(answers on last page)

Why didn't the Psychic laugh at any jokes?

Because he thought them all before.

How do you give a Psychic a surprise party?

You don't.

How many Psychics does it take to change a burnt out light bulb?

None. One Psychic can change a bulb, but it's before it's burnt out.

What do you get when you cross a Psychic with a bird?

A Psychic Bird

What do you get when you cross a Psychic with a gorilla?

A Psychic Gorilla

What do you get when you cross a Psychic with a reader?

How did you know that??? Are you psychic?

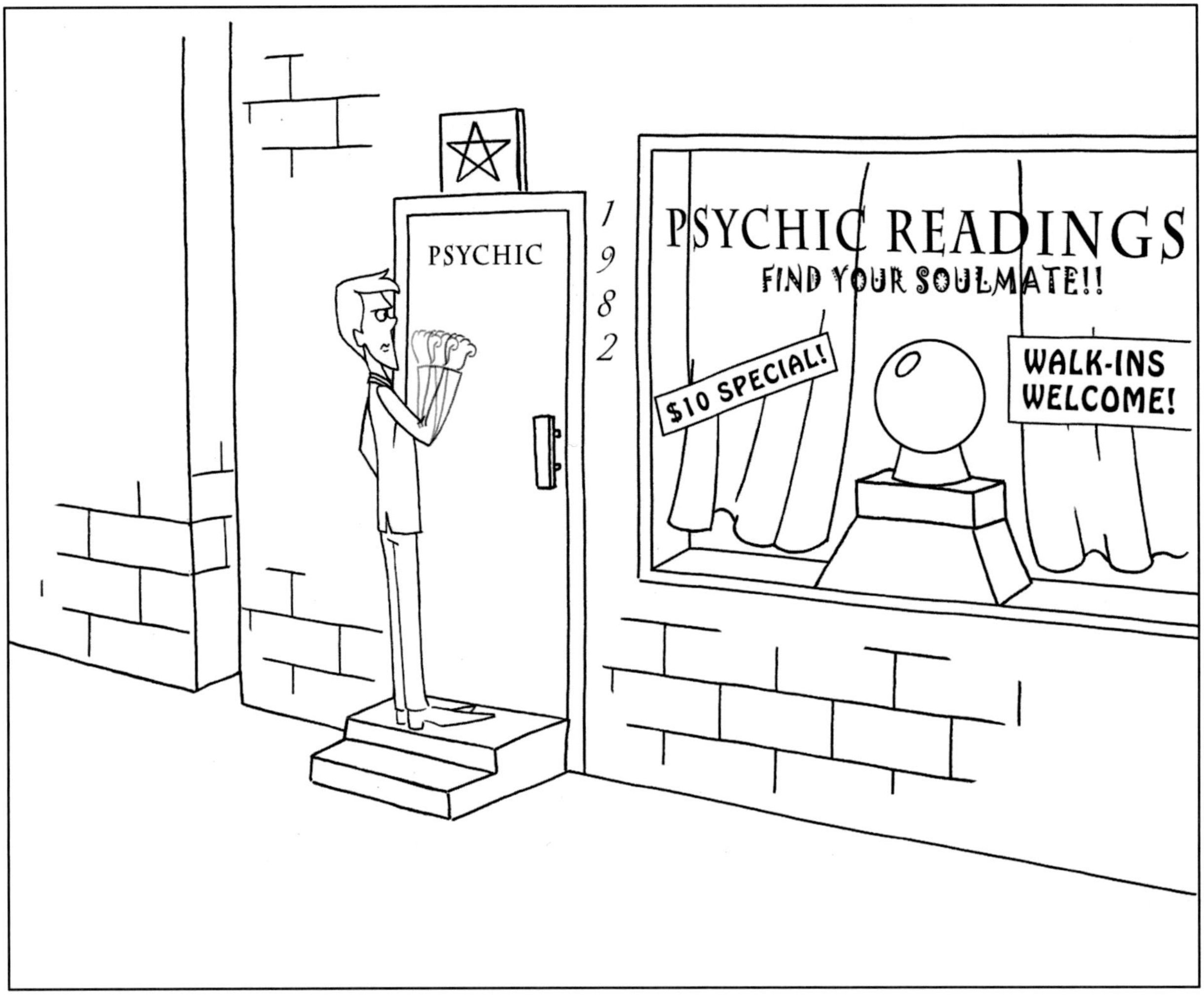
PSYCHIC
1982
PSYCHIC READINGS
FIND YOUR SOULMATE!!
$10 SPECIAL!
WALK-INS WELCOME!

KNOCK, KNOCK

Who's there?

Huh?!?

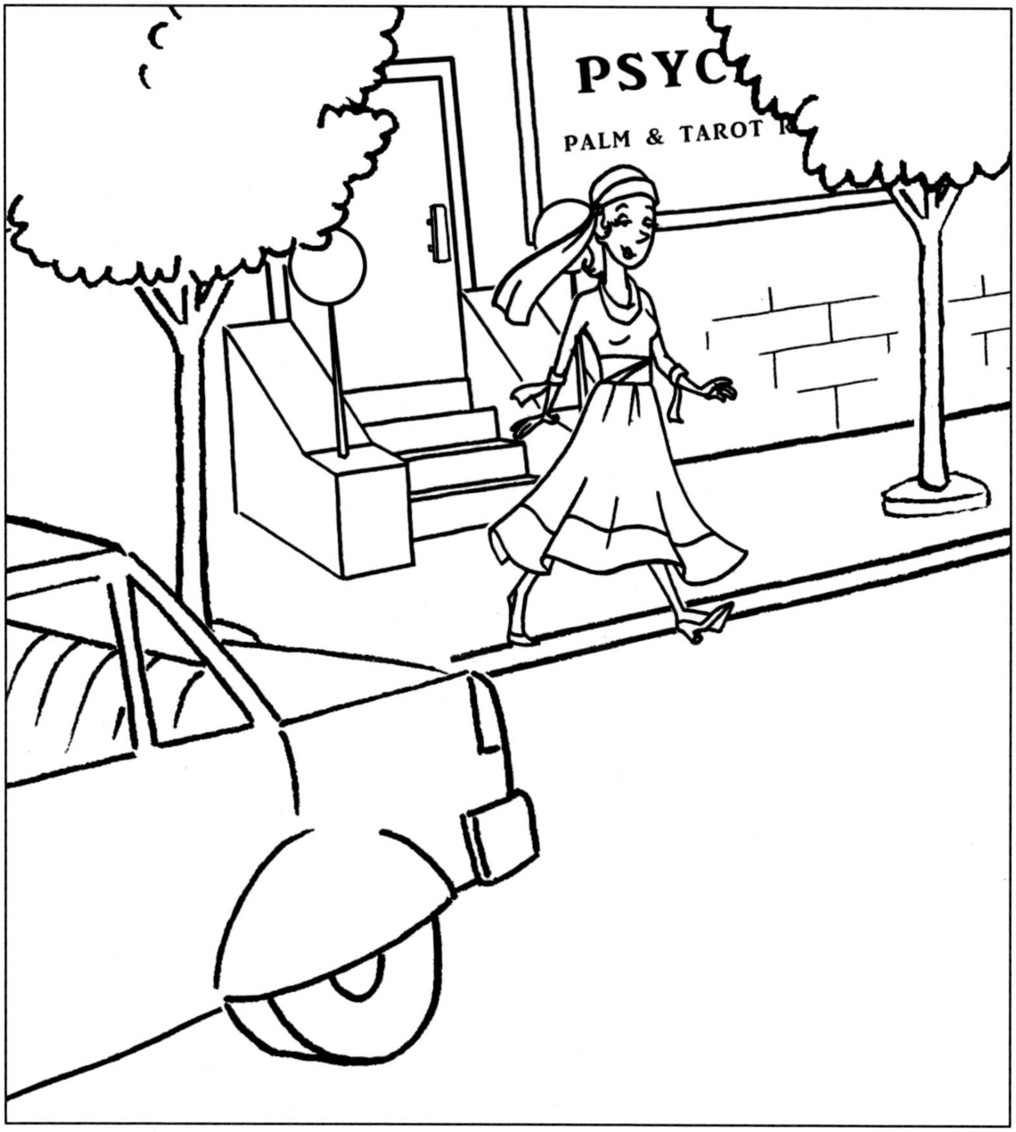
PSYC
PALM & TAROT R

Why did the Psychic cross the road?

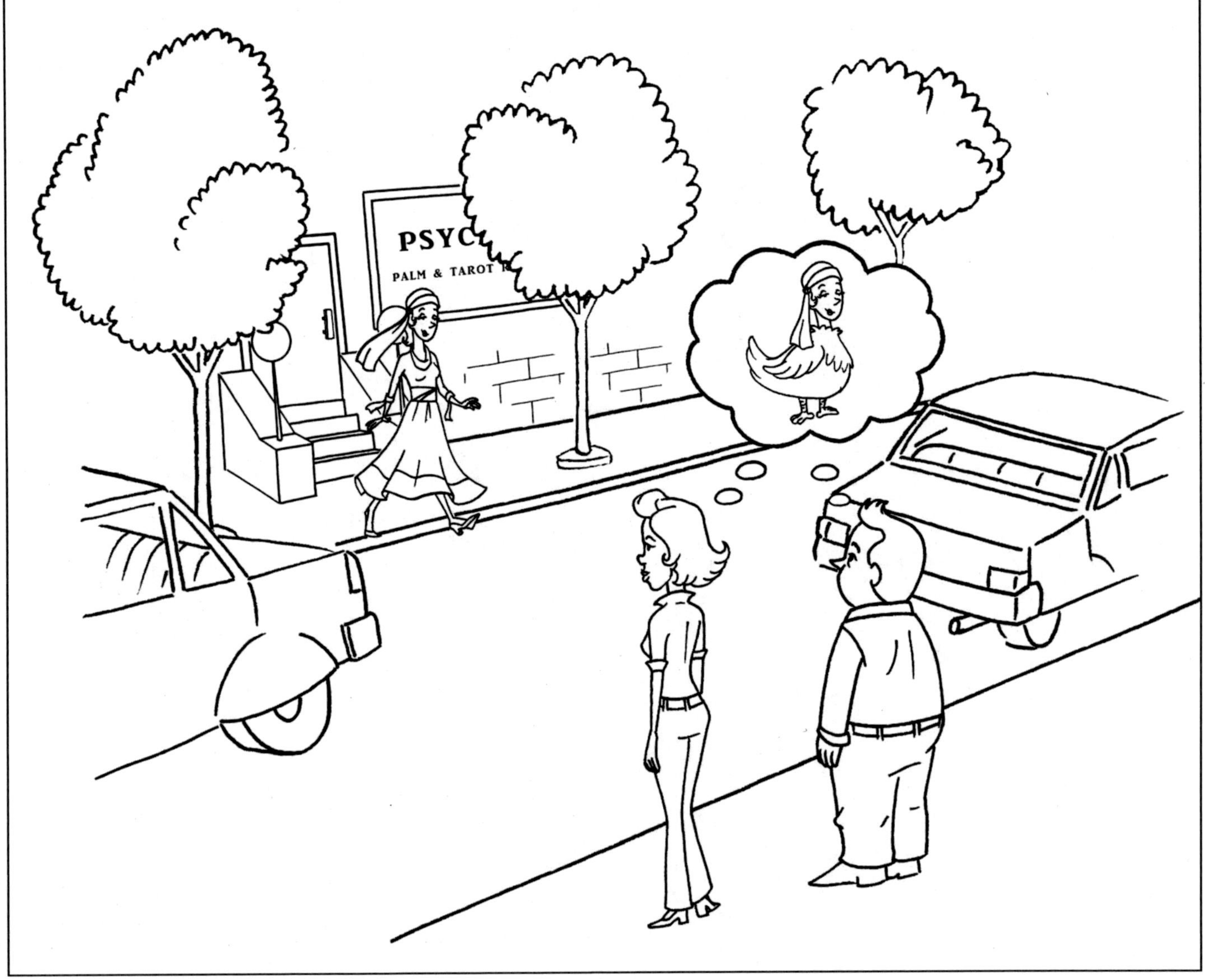
PSYC
PALM & TAROT

...Because her friends thought she was a chicken.

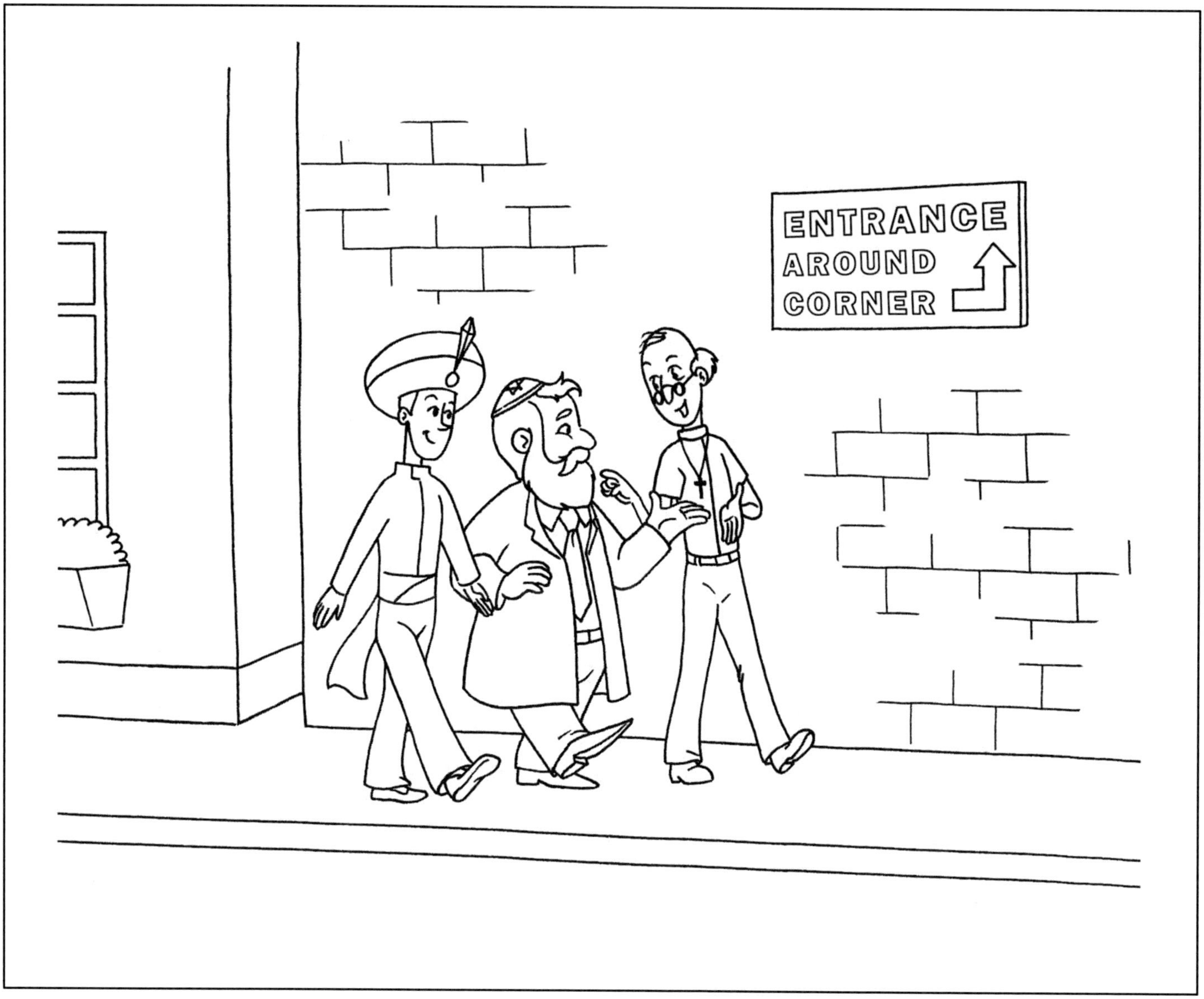
ENTRANCE
AROUND
CORNER

A Priest and a Rabbi walked into a bar...

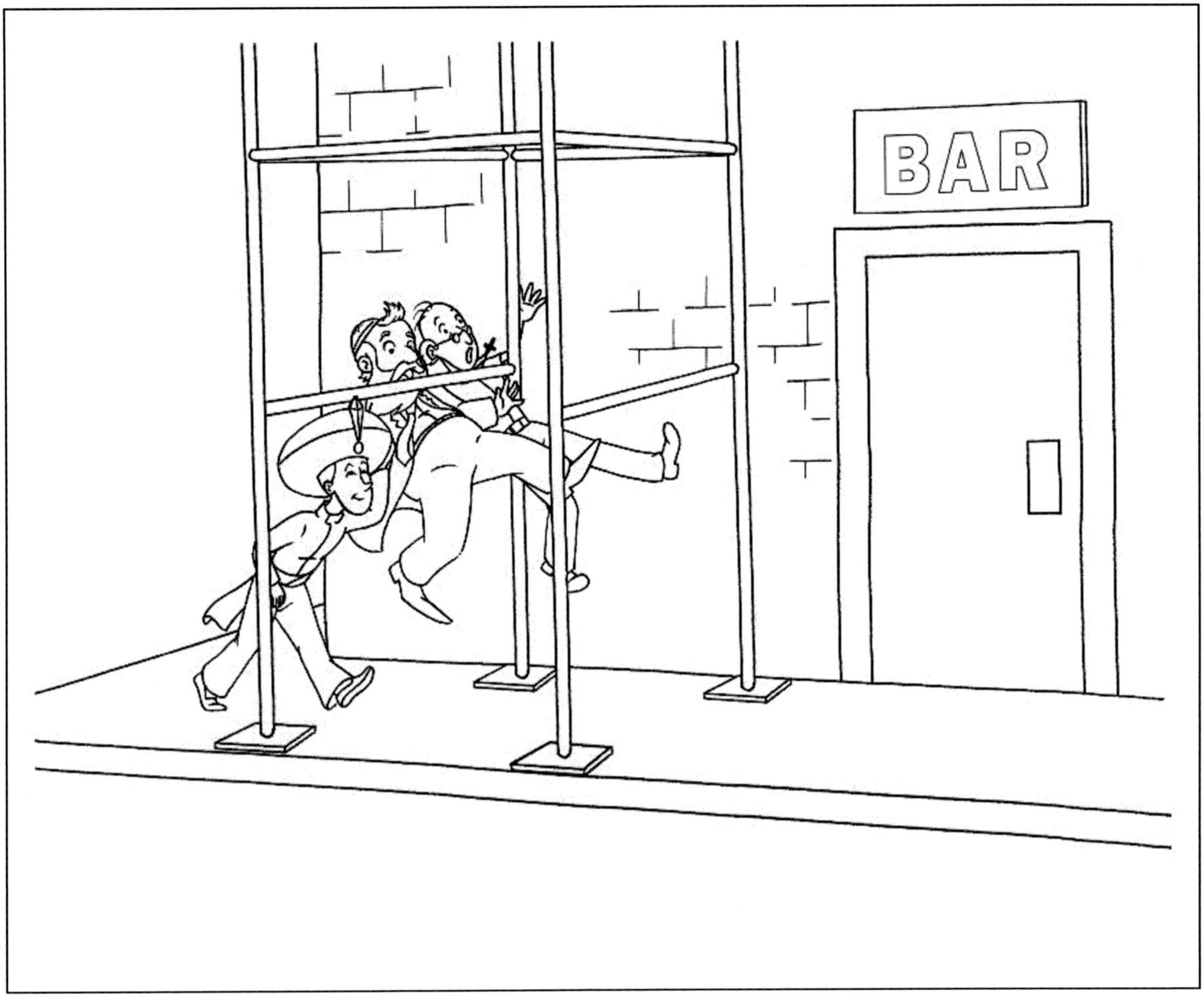
BAR

... the Psychic ducked.

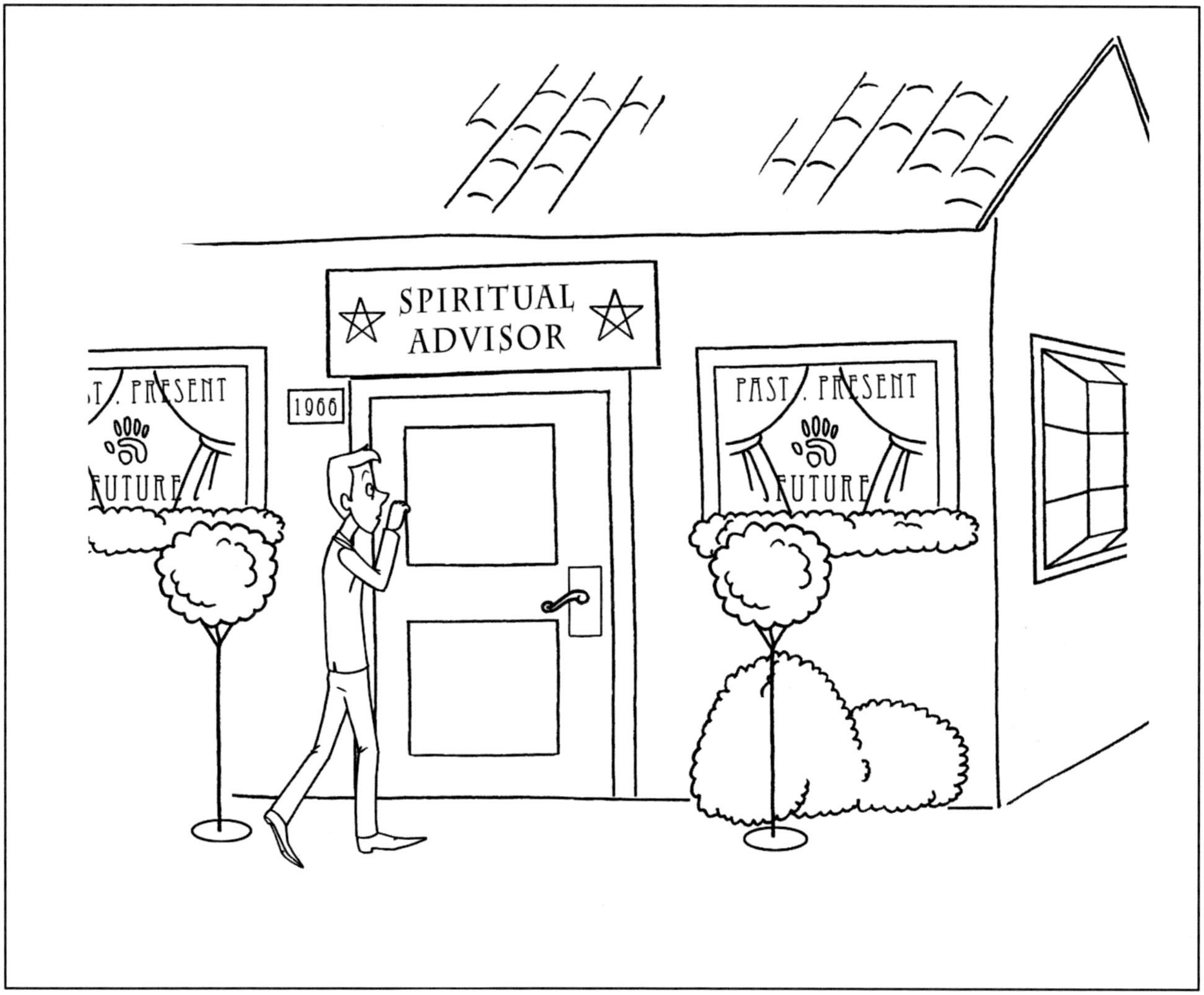
SPIRITUAL
ADVISOR
1966
PRESENT
FUTURE
PAST . PRESENT
FUTURE

Come on in, Joe!

For more adventures of ESPete®, read

ESPete®: Sixth Grade Sense

I know what you're thinking. It's some kind of trick. Well, that's what most of you are thinking at least. Kyle in Denver is thinking of the number seventeen. And Cindy in Tucson, well, you shouldn't be thinking about that for a few more years.

I'm sorry. How rude! For those of you who can't read minds, my name is Peter Powell. I'm eleven years old and the only child of Lawrence and Angela Powell of Urbana, Illinois. My dad is a professor at the University's computer lab. And my mom works at the public library. My parents are thinking of having another child, but they don't want to tell me and get my hopes up. Newsflash. No hopes here. I like getting all the attention.

I know it's hard to believe that I can read minds. Heck, it's hard to believe I can even read a book considering how poorly I was doing in English class up until this year.

I didn't realize why I was so distracted during quiet time until I was at the school psychologist's office in the beginning of sixth grade. Everyone at Jackson Middle School, Andrew not Michael, thought I had ADHD. Ms. Hornbauer freaked when I asked her what ADHD meant. She figured I must have overheard my parents talking about it. Oh, it stands for Attention Deficit Hyperactivity Disorder.

I started telling Ms. Hornbauer how I hear people talking when their lips aren't moving, and she suddenly got all weird. I mean, weirder than she already is. That's when I heard her thinking about testing me for ESP.

I was going to ask her what ESP stood for, but luckily she thought it. It's Extrasensory Perception, the ability to read minds or see the future, sometimes known as the sixth sense. I guess it would be the fifth for me, along with sight, hearing, taste and touch. I don't smell very well. I mean, my nose doesn't pick up smells very well. I don't stink, at least not anymore. I started using deodorant last year, and I shower once a week, whether I need it or not.

Anyhow, I got scared when Ms. Hornbauer began thinking about how we could go on talk shows together. I might have been excited if it was Mr. Stevens, the history teacher. He's cool. But I started getting images of driving all over America in Ms. Hornbauer's Volkswagen beetle. Everyone calls her the French Horn. She doesn't even speak French, so I think it's because of how she smells. I don't think she uses deodorant. I told her I heard about ADHD because I had listened to my parents talking. I know it's not right to lie, but it's also not right to make anyone ride all over the country with the French Horn.

Once I realized that all the other kids didn't hear everybody's thoughts, I started doing better in class, which was good. I was already nervous enough starting middle school.

Unfortunately, Rodney Bell was waiting to see the French Horn right after me. He was the biggest kid in school, even bigger than the eighth graders.

"Hey, E.S. Pete," Rodney yelled. "Hurry up! I don't have all day, dude."

Rodney had heard Ms. Hornbauer ask if I had ESP and thought it was funny. He was right. I was able to read his mind. He was also wrong. It wasn't funny. If you think someone likes being teased, think again.

Anyway, being psychic isn't all it's cracked up to be. Like, when I broke the lamp in my parent's bedroom. I knew I was going to be grounded for two weeks. Did that help me get out of it? Noooo! Another problem with reading minds is that it's not an exact science. I mean, I usually know what you're thinking at the moment, but that doesn't mean you won't change your mind. Or, that you're not wrong.

I learned that lesson the hard way when I tried to read Casey Grant's mind during our math test. She thought she was great at math. She thought wrong. Mrs. Johnson almost accused us of cheating because we both had the same exact incorrect answers. Luckily I sit across the room from Casey, so Mrs. Johnson knew we couldn't have looked at each other's papers. I don't see why it's cheating if I can read someone's mind. You're supposed to use your head to do the math and that's exactly what I did. How come it's not cheating if you're good at math and get a hundred percent?

I guess there are some good things about having ESP, though, especially in middle school. It's a tough time, trying to figure out what the world expects of you and what you expect of the world.

My parents always say not to worry too much, that "everyone else is just as confused as you are." Well, I happen to know that is true. Sometimes, they're even more confused. Especially when there's a school dance coming up. I wanted to ask Casey to go with me. I was just waiting for the right time.

www.espete.com

Read a Book, Read a Mind®

-DON'T PEAK-

SREWSNA ELZZUP

PSYCHIC CROSSWORD PUZZLE

F	I	N	G	E	R	S												
				S		E	A	R	S									
				P		N												
						S	I	G	H	T								
						O				A								
						R				S	M	E	L	L				
						Y				T					B	O	O	K
									M	E	D	I	U	M				
									I									
									N									
									D									

PSYCHIC WORD SEARCH

E	S	P	R	E	S	I	D	E	N	T
P	G	Y	Q	C	M	C	G	R	R	R
N	A	J	H	N	I	E	A	E	P	B
Y	Z	R	N	T	Y	H	D	S	Y	Z
E	E	N	A	M	A	A	C	I	E	L
S	D	N	J	N	E	P	E	Y	U	Y
P	Y	Y	D	R	O	S	E	L	S	M
R	B	L	D	O	P	R	M	L	G	P
L	L	N	M	E	R	B	M	V	E	Z
N	I	D	T	Q	P	R	P	A	Z	T
M	K	E	N	N	L	Y	W	J	L	X

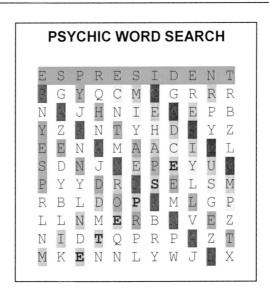

Puzzles made at Puzzle-Maker.com

Made in the USA
Middletown, DE
17 December 2015